SIZZLE AND
BURN

SIZZLE AND BURN

ALEXIS GRANT

St. Martin's Paperbacks

This is a work of fiction. All of the characters, organizations, and events portrayed in this novel are either products of the author's imagination or are used fictitiously.

SIZZLE AND BURN

Copyright © 2011 by Alexis Grant.
Excerpt from *Locked and Loaded* copyright © 2011 by Alexis Grant.

For information address St. Martin's Press, 175 Fifth Avenue, New York, NY 10010.

ISBN: 978-0-312-94303-5

Printed in the United States of America

St. Martin's Paperbacks edition / July 2011

St. Martin's Paperbacks are published by St. Martin's Press, 175 Fifth Avenue, New York, NY 10010.

10 9 8 7 6 5 4 3 2 1

May God bless those who serve. I want to thank all of the brave men and women who serve in the Armed Forces, who bravely put their lives and limbs in harm's way so that we can all enjoy the very expensive thing called freedom (something that we often take for granted). Freedom ain't free, and there are thousands of people who leave their families, loved ones, friends, and neighbors to serve. They give their lives, give up their personal interests, and go out there and do a job that I cannot even fathom having to do. I could not write this book without first thanking them.

But no book can really be complete without a "special forces" unit of experts and good friends.

Therefore I'd like to give Special Acknowledgement to:
Chip Armstrong and Phil Beaver, two graduates of the US Military Academy at West Point. Thank you, gentlemen, for always making sure I am procedurally correct (smile!). Also special thanks on the "military lingo." *Roger that!* I'd like to also thank my good buddy, Thomas Wims, for his invaluable tech consulting. But there was no way in the world that I'd be able to accurately and credibly navigate the streets of New York with el barrio flavor were it not for Carmen Perez—lady,

you are a walking encyclopedia. Thanks, You! And for the backup info in the BK, thank you, Adrienne King, Roshida Downey, Lisa Lanausse—you ladies rock! NYC Street Team in the houze and on-point! Last but not least in the "expert" category, THANK YOU, geologist Walt Stone, for getting me on the right track to let me know if my plot was even plausible. Dude . . . I'm just sayin', WOW, LOL!

I would also like to thank my editor, Rose Hilliard, who was a true gem and the vanguard of patience as I researched and got this to her. Thanks for being such a doll . . . and of course there's Sara Crowe, my agent, who walks on water as far as I'm concerned. BIG HUG!

PROLOGUE

The Azores . . .

Nine hundred miles off the coast of Portugal and half an ocean away from home, the memories came drifting back. The light breeze coming in from the sea seemed to clear his head and momentarily blew away any thoughts of death and assassination, bringing Mia into his mind like a phantom caress.

Vibrant hibiscus climbed from the heavy clay urns that dotted the quaint São Miguel sidewalk café. People strolled by at a leisurely pace; beautiful women talked with their hands, preening like summer birds. He watched them all, saw them all, cataloging each person by rote—seeing them without seeing them.

Despite his mission, it was impossible to sit among the bright-hued blooms and watch all the tourist couples walk by and not remember that, the last time he'd seen Mia, the cherry blossoms at the National Arboretum in DC were raining down pink confetti on her pretty auburn hair. Paradise always got to him. It was better to be lying in jungle mud or hunkered down in a sandstorm than to be in a place like this where it was too easy to mentally conjure up Mia. But the U.S. Army's 1st Special Forces Operational Detachment—Delta didn't give him that choice.

Regardless, ten years was too long to still want every inch of someone who was gone . . . Her satin-smooth caramel skin, her light floral scent . . . her whispers. He remembered all of her as though he'd been with her last night. Paradise had a way of doing that to a man, had a way of haunting him beyond rum drinks and exotic women. But none of them was her.

Right now time was killing him. It was decimating his concentration, slipping between the cracks of the present and making him think back to the past, back to something that couldn't be recovered. He'd been waiting nearly two hours, pretending to read the newspaper while enjoying his cafezinho, and thinking of her. It was a dangerous combination to be in the midst of a negotiation and to have his mind wander.

Ryan took a very slow, steady sip from his coffee cup, wresting his attention back to the prime directive and visually surveying the passersby. Only Americans gobbled down their breakfasts or ate while walking and driving, and then went on with their day. In foreign countries it was easier to wait uninterrupted or unsuspected. No one ever seemed in a rush. But where was his contact?

Trade winds caught the edge of his mind along with the edge of his newspaper as he set it down on the table next to his abandoned plate. The scent of the sea was in the air. Seemed like yesterday that a gentle breeze had created pink whirls of cast-away blossoms that blew over Mia's sandals. She'd been delighted, and that had made him smile. Mia had pretty feet. She'd laughed as the errant blooms caught between her tiny pink polished toes. She was the only woman he knew whose feet were as soft as her hands. Her smile always captivated him, just like her large, beautiful brown eyes.

Then out of the blue, like a flash downpour in early spring—and just as quickly as she'd offered an upturned pout with a giggle in a way that ran all through him—her mood changed. Her expression became serene, then intense and seeking, making him want her. They'd made love that afternoon like a hard, clean rain, one that was sudden and unrelenting.

Mia . . .

To him, even her name was synonymous with spring, that season of anticipation. But that was a long time ago. By now a woman that fine would be married with children, he reasoned, and then jettisoned the bittersweet memory.

Captain Ryan Mason studied the terrain from behind a pair of dark aviator sunglasses and then took another sip of cafezinho. With his five o'clock shadow, a four-inch thicket of natural twists, a racer's bike leaning against the tree by his table, and green-and-yellow biker's shorts and T-shirt adding contrast to his dark walnut skin, he looked like a Brazilian tourist on holiday.

For all the body-hardening training he'd endured in an elite Ranger battalion before being recruited to Special Forces, he was glad that Delta Force didn't require counterinsurgency units to do the clean-shaven, crew-cut routine. That would have been a dead giveaway on a mission designed for a quick surgical strike while maintaining the lowest possible profile of U.S. involvement.

Some asshole was gonna die today, or set off a chain of events over his dead body.

Finally, a very frail and frightened little man skittered out from the hotel across the street. Ryan tensed. The man's thin brown body was drawn wire-taut, and he kept dabbing sweat from his brow and the horseshoe bald spot in the center of his head. Quickly sizing him up, Ryan knew it was his Pakistani contact. He waved the server over and ordered another coffee so that they could dispense with that interruption when the professor arrived at his table.

"Good morning," the professor said, and then sat across from Ryan in jerky, halting movements. He looked three ways like a nervous ferret and then leaned in as Ryan calmly brought his cafe-zinho to his lips. "My family and I are here now, vacationing . . ."

"You look flushed, Professor. Are you hot? The weather is warm today."

"No . . . no . . . I'm just fine, thank you."

Ryan waited for the man to answer the obscure question the way he'd been instructed—if he was hot, wearing a wire, then Ryan would have to figure out a new way to have a conversation with him. The professor had been told to blink once for yes, blink twice for no to indicate whether or not he was being monitored by the other side. As though suddenly remembering the code, the professor leaned forward, released a little gasp, and then blinked twice.

As discreetly as possible, Ryan coolly slid a hotel room key across the table within the folded newspaper that the man greedily snatched up. He waited until the professor held the paper up, pretended to peruse the headlines as the key dropped into his lap beneath the table, and then he eased it into his pants beneath the buckle so that no one could see the key exchange.

"Good," Ryan said. "After we have our coffee and chat, you'll be met in your new room. Arrangements have been made for your amnesty in exchange for vital intel. Our unit is poised to burn whoever is holding your family. We do extractions all the time, and just need to know where they are in the building. But screw up, and we don't know you or your family. Save a hundred thousand lives, then the enemy of our enemy is our friend." Ryan placed his cell phone on the table next to his saucer. "One phone call is your lifeline—or not."

The professor swallowed hard and nodded obediently, keeping his voice low after he'd cleared his throat. "They've set up a series of subaquatic depth charges to simultaneously explode. This archipelago is volcanic and covers nine islands and three hundred and fifty miles, but is only twenty-four hundred miles from the eastern United States. That means a tsunami hitting the East Coast is a frighteningly possible outcome. Finding where each bomb is strategically located will be impossible without my assistance . . . and with loose nuclear warhead munitions confiscated by the wrong hands from Russia's occupation in Afghanistan, even if you were to avert the tsunami they are attempting to create, you would still have a serious dilemma—no?"

There was no denying it: Without knowing exactly where the warheads were being placed, searching for them over the vast terrain would be like searching for a needle in a haystack. Timing was everything, and the clock was ticking. If the sick bastards set off a riptide of underwater explosions that destabilized the volcanic infrastructure of this island network, the tsunami created in the Azores would lash the East Coast with a natural disaster that could take incalculable numbers of lives. New

York City would suffer the brunt of the catastrophe, with most of Manhattan submerged. And Ryan couldn't even begin to fathom the level of damage a nuke could create.

Ryan watched his contact's small, bright eyes as they blinked behind his horn-rimmed glasses. Silver tufts of hair sprang up over his scalp and his wild black-and-gray eyebrows seemed to fuse into a thick, caterpillar-like center unibrow, giving the professor a truly insane countenance.

"How many loose nukes?" Ryan leaned on the table on his elbows, clasping his hands together to keep from choking the man before him to death.

"Just one. But the other warheads will be detonated with it . . . they've connected submarine torpedoes to it."

"And you have the maps to where they're going to place them?"

"Yes, the boats go out tonight. Six in all. It will happen in the darkness." The professor nodded quickly and then looked around, dropping his voice to an urgent whisper. "They forced me to tell them how to do this. They held my wife hostage for three days. I don't even know who these people are!"

Tears shimmered in the old man's eyes. Ryan remained impassive while the professor pressed on, becoming more distraught as he spoke, and now beginning to gesture with his hands.

"I am not your enemy. I would have to give up all that I know, hide like a common criminal now because of these people—and yet I have done nothing wrong. They could still kill me after they do this horrible thing to be sure there are no witnesses. Yet, in fear for the lives of my family, I have told them where to place the explosives for maximum effect. But to be sure I'm not lying to them they want me to monitor the process. That's why I can tell you where I am to meet them, where they'll have the monitoring stations, and where and when the detonation is to take place."

"And they just let you walk across the street to talk to me," Ryan said evenly, and then paused as a new cup of cafezinho was set before the professor. He waited for the server to leave before resuming in a low, monotone voice. "My bet is that you're already a dead man walking. They probably have two snipers on you and me as we speak."

"Yes. This is true. My life is at risk just meeting you now . . . I told them I needed to check with a younger colleague from the university about my hypothesis—someone trustworthy but more knowledgeable in the newer technologies. I told them that, to keep you unsuspecting, I would pretend to you that I was working on a paper for a journal so that I could participate in the Global Earthquake and Volcanic Activity Conference happening in New York City this week. That is the only reason they've allowed me to come out to have breakfast with you. The things that go on in places where there is no stability, you cannot imagine. This is not what I studied for, or what I gave my life to research . . . this is an abomination. I am ashamed, but I have children, a wife . . . what was I to do?"

"Where is your family?"

"Out by the pool, making it seem as though they are fine to all onlookers. But they are being guarded by a man with a hidden gun. He sits right out there with them as though he is my family!"

The professor drew a shuddering breath as two large tears rolled down the bridge of his nose. "Please save them, even if you cannot help me. If this terrorist act gets stopped here in the Azores, these fanatics will only find another professor—someone else like me who is innocent but has knowledge. They are relentless. That is why I was so afraid . . . afraid enough to tell them the truth. But now I see that being honest has not only left me and my family still at risk, but could take the lives of so many others. How could I sleep at night knowing that all my research to avert world disasters would actually be used to create one? It is a cruel and horrible irony. Please . . ."

The professor's words trailed off as he hung his head and drew in a thick, mucus-filled wheeze.

"You take a few sips of coffee, then go back into the hotel—but do not go to the pool. Go to the room I gave you the key for. Understood? If you don't follow my explicit instructions, your family's blood will be on your hands."

The professor bit his lip to stifle a sob. Then he nodded.

Ryan slowly picked up the cell phone, pressed the number linked to speed dial, and then said two words. "He's legit."

CHAPTER 1

Washington, DC...

Mia walked up the steps of the Smithsonian National Museum of Natural Science, but stopped for a moment to marvel at the profusion of cherry blossoms that dotted the landscape. The city had finally climbed out of the long, bleak winter that had paralyzed it with brutal snowstorms and icy highways.

This time of year DC was awash in pink splendor. Witnessing the delicate beauty always gave her pause, as well as the stinging reminder that sometimes something so beautiful could also be ephemeral. Try as she might, and as much as she hated to allow the old memories to bathe her like the warm morning sunlight, there was no escaping her thoughts of Ryan during this time of year.

Even after a brief but turbulent engagement to

another man that was fraught with career jealousy, the decade-old memory of Ryan Mason still haunted her.

What they'd shared was fast, intense, and damned near insane. Theirs was a spring that flowered suddenly, beautifully, and was gone before they'd hardly had a chance to catch their breaths. The breakup had nothing to do with incompatibility, bickering, or infidelity, like the relationships she'd experienced since that magical spring. It was simply that they'd both made irrevocable choices, then.

A light breeze lifted her ponytail and caught the front edges of her hair, making it spill out from beneath her faux-tortoiseshell headband. Ryan used to gently smooth back her hair, tucking strays wisps behind her ear just before he'd bring his lips to hers. Mia briefly closed her eyes and adjusted the sash on her Burberry raincoat—an extravagance she'd allowed herself when she'd successfully completed her dissertation—then hiked up her Coach briefcase on her shoulder—a gift from her mother upon graduation. She released a small wistful sigh, remembering, as she watched a few lone blooms blow across the pavement beyond the steps.

Thirty-one years old, with all the education in the world, making forty-seven thousand dollars a year on a postdoctoral fellowship . . . and no man . . . no children . . . no prospects. This was not how she'd envisioned her life, even though her entire family viewed her as the poster girl for success. Yes, she'd made all the right educational and career moves and was tracking to have a very solid future, but what about the gaps and holes in her everyday existence? What about laughter and happiness and some of the hard-to-describe intangibles, like love? Ryan Mason was probably a general by now, she mused, and then shunted the thought away. And probably married with beautiful children or in love and happy. It wasn't her business. The past was dead and buried, she told herself. What did it matter, anyway?

Fate had a cruel sense of humor; it gave with one hand while it took away with the other. She'd been granted a full fellowship at Cornell University after a summa cum laude performance at Vassar. Immediately following his graduation from West Point, Ryan was commissioned as a second lieutenant of Infantry and headed to Infantry Officer Basic Course at Fort Benning, Georgia, after only two weeks of leave.

There was no time, save that glorious, intoxicating two weeks of promises followed by his three weeks of Airborne School, immediately followed by nine weeks in the grueling, elite U.S. Army Ranger School—then a demanding first year in the 82nd Airborne Division as a rifle platoon leader at Fort Bragg that included deployments all over God knew where.

A yellow school bus that brought in girls from the surrounding colleges had brought them together, and dreams and ambition ultimately drove them apart. Neither could relent. How could two kids, one from Bed-Stuy and one from Spanish Harlem, ask the other to give up on their dreams, especially after having fought so hard to get out of their neighborhoods?

Pulling herself away from the past and determined to get mentally settled before entering the building, Mia watched small birds quarrel and then take flight from the blossom-laden branches. She remembered feeling what it was like to fly.

A minority academic scholarship got her to Vassar; heavy recruitment to play football, a chance to play Division One level at that, and a full ride for college with a salary, too, got him to West Point. From there it seemed as though the sky was the limit. They'd found each other, had found out that life held infinite possibilities . . . found out that they could have it all . . . maybe just not all at the same time.

They'd lost contact while he was in Ranger School. Back then, nine weeks felt like nine years. There'd be no letters or phone calls while he was cut off from the outside world. A chance internship for her to study seismology for a semester in Indonesia, then an internship in Yellowstone National Park sealed their fate. The distance and lack of communication was just too much. That was the thing: you could never go back. Like her abuela always said, "Once the egg is broke, the egg is broke."

Mia pushed past the memory with an impatient huff of breath and walked up the steps and into the building. Henry Jackson, the elderly security guard there, greeted her with his customary wide smile.

"Good morning, *Dr.* Austin," he said, tipping his hat and beaming at her. His voice was filled with pride as he added extra emphasis to her title. The vicarious pleasure he took from her success was palpable—it had been that way since the day they'd met. Now their warm, coded greetings were an unspoken dance performed every morning and every evening without fail.

"Good morning to you, Mr. Jackson," she replied brightly, giving him back the cheer he'd so generously offered her as she swiped her badge across the security gate. His smile felt like a touch of home and was so sorely needed right now. His wise eyes made her linger just long enough to offer a bit of small talk. "It's so pretty out today. Pink is everywhere."

"Indeed it is . . . blossoms probably came out just for you." He gave her a jaunty nod as though confirming his theory as fact. "You have a very nice day and stay blessed, Doctor."

"You, too, Mr. Jackson."

Mia watched the crinkles around the older man's eyes deepen as he stood up a little taller when she passed him. No one else called him by his last name, much less put the respectful *Mr.* around the acknowledgment. But to a man who was easily her

mother's senior, she knew a simple gesture like
that meant the world.

She frowned but kept facing the elevators when
she heard one of her co-workers enter behind her
and hail Mr. Jackson as Henry. Yet Mr. Jackson
had called her co-worker Dr. Lewis. Mia cringed
inwardly. Would it have killed Josh to call the old
man by his full and righteous title? She also didn't
want to turn around to see the defeated deference
she knew would be in Mr. Jackson's eyes once Josh
had passed him. She'd seen it in her abuela growing up and hated to see it in any brown-hued elderly eyes.

Sometimes she'd go with her grandmother when
her abuela used to travel all the way from Spanish
Harlem to clean other people's houses and watch
other people's children. They called her Isabel,
never Mrs. Martinez, even when she used their
titles and surnames as a gesture of respect. Mia
learned early on that such slights were part of her
reality as a half African American, half Latina . . .
a "blatina" as they said back home.

It brought her a measure of comfort to know
that, like Mr. Jackson, her parents and all her aunts,
uncles, and cousins took pride in her degree as
though they'd earned it themselves. Maybe by ex-
tension, her abuela and Mr. Jackson had. Maybe
her entire family had. It was the one thing that kept
her going. Mr. Jackson's quiet, daily reaffirmation

that a lot of people were looking up to her kept her going.

Rankled, Mia pretended not to see Josh as he rushed forward when she entered the elevator, but he unfortunately caught it.

"Hey," Josh said, forcing the doors to open for him.

"Oh . . . hey, Josh. Didn't see you," she said blandly, trying to chase the annoyance out of her tone. "Sorry."

"No biggie," he said, and then took an exaggerated slurp of his Starbucks coffee and pushed the button for their floor. "Heard old man Cortland is letting you assist on the presentation in New York. I sure am glad they didn't rope me into doing it."

It was just like Josh to add another layer of stress to a situation that was already secretly freaking her out. He was such a competitive little weasel. Mia just stared at him for a moment as the elevator doors closed.

"I'm ready for it," she finally replied, summoning a way to block him out of her mind. She felt entombed with Joshua Lewis standing so close and invading her personal space. If he didn't back up, a Spanish Harlem flare might erupt within her like a sunspot flash. He had to get out of her face. But rather than go there, Mia backed up, feigning the need to find a mint in her purse.

"Well, I sure hope so—because you know this is either a chance to shine or really leave a career stain. Whew . . . I don't know if I could take the pressure. Everybody is going to be there in New York, and I mean *everybody*."

Mia stared at the slowly ascending numbers as they lit on the elevator panel. Joshua Lewis was *such* a social irritant, and this was just another of his blatant attempts to undermine her.

"And you're getting to *actually present*," he continued. Do you know how huge that is? With everything that's been going on recently with natural disasters and with the White House's focus on them, all papers and presentations will get high visibility. International visibility. *Career make-or-break visibility*."

Joshua hesitated, taking another deep slurp of his coffee as he stared at her from behind his thick horn-rimmed glasses. "You know, we're both here on this grueling twelve-month fellowship in earth and planetary sciences that doesn't pay jack. So it's like we're sorta in the trenches together, right? We've gotta watch each other's backs, professionally. I wouldn't mind helping a colleague, especially a beautiful one."

So that was his plan—to horn in on her presentation, and possibly in on her. This was a conversation she so didn't want to have. The elevator sounded, and for her it was a bell of salvation. Forcing a smile and civility into her tone, she quickly gave Joshua a sidelong glance, focusing on his pocket protector as the elevator doors opened. "Thanks so much, Josh. I'll definitely keep that in mind." Then she bolted.

"But the summit is tomorrow!" he called behind her. "I can come over to your place tonight, if you want, so we can pull an all-nighter. I don't have plans."

"I'll text you if I get into trouble," she said over her shoulder, hastening her pace toward her mentor's office. "But thanks. Gotta go."

It took everything within her not to break into a flat-out dash down the corridor to escape. The Division of Petrology and Volcanology, just like the Department of Mineral Sciences' Division of Seismology, used to be one of her sanctuaries. However, since she'd mysteriously removed her engagement ring six months ago and wouldn't talk about it beyond saying "It didn't work out," and Dr. Cortland had announced that she'd be co-presenting with him at the Global Earthquake and Volcanic Activity Conference—not only had she been evading dating inquiries from on-the-job suitors, but she'd also been fending off professional encroachment on her project.

Quickly waving at her colleagues as she passed their cubicles, Mia made a beeline to Dr. Cortland's office, one that the Smithsonian generously allowed him to keep as their inducement to have him stay on well beyond his retirement. By the time she'd reached his secretary's desk, she was almost winded.

"Hi, Mia. Good morning. He's in there." The older woman smiled at her as she peered over the tops of her glasses and smoothed back the edges of her graying blond bun. She then sent her merry blue gaze around Mia's body to peer down the corridor and bit her lip, holding back a full smile for a moment before dropping her voice to a conspiratorial whisper. "And you'd better get in there quick before Josh comes up with yet another reason why he should go to the conference in Dr. Cortland's suitcase."

Mia laughed, and that finally made Hannah's restraint crumble. Theirs was a relationship forged by mutual agreement to drop the formality, a decision made day one. It was so simple a thing that sealed their bond. Mia had addressed the older woman as Mrs. Wiseman, and she'd replied, "Oh, don't be silly. Call me Hannah." That was all it took. But the small attempt at civility had endeared Mia to the older woman. From then on, Hannah looked out for Mia as though she were a daughter.

"Oh, my God, Hannah, and good morning to you, too," Mia said, blowing out a hard breath through a very bad case of the giggles. "The guy is relentless."

Hannah waved her hand as though shooing away a gnat. "You're telling me?" She shook her head and gave Mia a wink. "And don't let him scare you—your presentation is fine without him. He's been lobbying Dr. Cortland to let him assist you, as though you need *his* help. Please."

"He went to Dr. Cortland behind my back?" Mia's giggles faded as she stood before Hannah stupefied.

Hannah nodded. "But you didn't hear that from me. It really ruffled Ian, though. He hates sneaks. So Josh only hurt himself with that little back-alley move."

"Wow . . . ," Mia murmured, surprised but then again not.

"Just remember why Ian chose you for this honor. He knows your work, your attention to detail, and he knows you've worked hard with him for years and *deserve* for people to know who you are. Break a leg."

"Thanks, Hannah," Mia said in a quiet tone and then slipped past her to knock on her mentor's door.

"Come in, come in," Ian Cortland called out, but before Mia could put her hand on the knob, the door opened. "Good morning, my dear. How is my favorite research fellow?"

"Good morning, sir. I'm having a case of acid reflux brought on by this opportunity, but I'll survive."

He issued her a lopsided grin as he ushered her into his office and shut the door behind them. "I figured as much. Oh, I threw up right before my first major presentation. I hate public speaking—did I ever tell you that? Well, it's half the reason why I'm sending you out there." He gave her a wink and then chuckled. "But the *real* reason is because *you're damned good.* Today is T-minus-twenty-four-hours till you make your debut. A case of nerves is only normal."

Dr. Ian Cortland stood in front of her, a robust five feet, six inches' worth of tireless energy. She looked down at him with a warm smile of appreciation. His white beard was a mangy confection about his face, and the tufts of silvery white hair on his head stubbornly rimmed a gleaming, rose-tinted bald spot in the center of it. He wore a light blue sweater that suffered from lint and strained over his belly, with a dingy, white oxford buttondown shirt that needed a good starching and was open at the collar. His Dockers pants were rumpled; his penny loafers were in sore need of a resole and good shine. But the man's brilliance and warmth of spirit made all that invisible to Mia.

Small gray eyes blinked at her with curiosity behind round wire frames, and the slight scent of pipe tobacco in the room suggested that he'd either violated the institution's rules about smoking inside the building or just come in from indulging one of his vices. You could never tell with Ian Cortland.

With a wave of his hand he gestured for her to sit down, and now inside the safe sanctuary of his office, she leisurely set down her bag and removed her coat. Dressed in a simple camel-hued sweater, black slacks, and flats, she plopped down in the chair facing his wide, walnut desk and crossed her legs. He sat on the edge of his desk and peered down at her. Instant relaxation washed over Mia. This was an old ritual, a comforting one between mentor and protégée—he would speak, she would soak in his wisdom and then go a step farther on her own in a way that would please him.

"You know," he said, leaning forward and stroking his beard. "We old codgers look for someone like you our entire careers . . . someone who can continue our work long after we're gone. Someone who can take our concepts to the next level and make a difference. Mia, you are that special brand of scientist—one who, yes, has great analytical skill, but who also feels the data with gut instinct in a way that cannot be taught. Your hunches take you down paths that pure research alone may not uncover for years."

He nodded as she looked away, humbled and pleased by his compliment. "Tell you a little secret," he pressed on, but waited until their eyes met again. "The older I get, the more I'm finding that science is part data and part hunch, and the nexus of the two is the true art of the science." He hopped down off his desk to begin pacing by the window with his hands behind his back. "It's heresy, I know, to speak this way—and I'd never do it publicly . . . well, maybe I would. At this juncture, who cares, right?"

He looked at her and chuckled as her smile widened. "But I'll wait to be esoteric and eclectic after your debut as not to tarnish the shine on my new rising star. It is true, though. Try not to forget that as you take your research deeper."

"I promise," she said, struggling not to laugh as she waited for his big reveal. At every session, he'd give her a nugget of knowledge, a kernel of his genius to take home and nurse. It was a gift that she'd always bring back wrapped in something special that she'd found for him.

"Good," he said, now pruning his window plants. "This living planet is changing—no secret. The earth is tired. We've sped things up, heated it up. Also no secret. We're pulling out this living entity's blood with our addiction to oil. That's changing the pressure beneath the mantle, all while we're seriously disturbing the electromagnetic fields with our power grids and pollution constructs. Never before have humans built cities of the population densities we see today . . . and we are arrogant enough to have built them in the paths of active volcanoes and on shifting tectonic plates—as though our pittance of technology could stop catastrophic events, if Mother Earth decides to burp or fart. It's madness. Look at what a relatively small volcanic eruption in Iceland did to air traffic in Europe. The entire system was grounded! That alone should be a wake-up call, without even counting all the catastrophes we've seen in recent history."

"I know . . . ," she said quietly, watching her mentor whip himself into a familiar rant. "But this conference—"

"May or may not get their attention," he said, wheeling around and cutting her off. "We have the mindless saying that the president's attempt to round up loose nukes is making our country weaker! We have people out there who run our Senate and our Congress who are talking about adding more of that poison to our world rather than blending it down to low-grade, fuel-level plutonium. We have people who couldn't give a rat's ass about a so-called third-world country experiencing an earthquake disaster, as long as it's over there—like it's on some other planet—because they are so ignorant of science and basic geology that they don't understand that it's *all connected*!"

"Dr. Cortland, I know that it seems like a futile exercise, but maybe now that forty-nine world leaders have come together on the nuclear arms issue, they'll also see how we have to be ready for all sorts of disasters of that magnitude."

"Maybe. But we've still got people walking around with picket signs and so-called news pundits saying that climate change and global warming are a sham." He shook his head and ran his palm over his bald spot. "It's like we're experiencing a second Dark Ages or something. For all the technology we have, men and women are selling their souls for the price of silver at the expense of scientific fact for television ratings—and *that*, Mia, is *medieval*!"

"True, but forty-nine world leaders made history this spring . . . for the first time in decades, they came together over an issue that used to be a bone of contention fueling the arms race."

Dr. Cortland held up his hands before his chest and sighed with a smile. "The optimism of youth keeps me from having a heart attack when I read *The Washington Post.* Thank you, Mia, for allowing me to vent."

They shared a chuckle as he returned to his desk. But then his mood sobered as he gazed at her thoughtfully.

"Mia, your work is going to blow them away. The whole theory of how many densely populated metropolitan areas sit upon the latticework of major faults—and man's ability to use those faults in conjunction with our weaponry to bring about catastrophic events—is pivotal to this conference. Unfortunately, humanity has never had as much power to self-annihilate as we do now. That must be as much a part of this conference on earthquakes and volcanoes as is studying the natural planetary changes taking place."

"After 9/11," Mia said in a reverent tone, "I realized that people only pay attention to what can immediately affect them. I knew that whoever did this was still out there wanting to do more harm and wouldn't stop until they hit New York or another major city again. They simply got too much mileage out of that first horrific strike. And say what you want, we're still wide open and vulnerable in our tunnels, our rail systems, you name it."

"Right you are," he said, nodding. "And with the recent rapid succession of severe quakes that hit Haiti, then Chile, Baja California and Mexico, then northern Sumatra, we have people's attention—and your theory has a chance to gain traction, Mia. New York City, Manhattan in particular, is vulnerable on the heels of the Haiti disaster, and it sits on top of six major faults. Because the conference is taking place in New York, yours will be one of those high-impact presentations that will no doubt garner you a lot of ink and a lot of speaking engagements, especially on the topic of utilizing natural disasters as a tool of terrorism. I would have never thought to add that twist to it, but that was a stroke of public relations genius for our cause of getting people to pay attention to the earth's evolution."

CHAPTER 2

The Azores . . .

The sun never had a chance to kiss the horizon before boots on the ground kicked in doors and shattered plans as though they were bone fragments. Flawless choreography as precise as a Swiss watch pulled women and children to safety before they even had a chance to scream, while snipers quietly dropped kidnappers with silenced bullets. Bodies and blood disappeared quickly, tourists being none the wiser.

In and out: No diplomatic dilemmas.

Cold sweat covered Ryan's body. Bursts of adrenaline threatened to make his limbs tremble. Cordite stained the air and left a sulfuric aftertaste in his mouth. But he was far from done.

Red laser dots on foreheads and chests promised seventy-two virgins would meet some men soon.

This was a take-no-prisoners mission, for none would allow themselves to be taken. Strategic backup from military intelligence with specialized linguistic skills kept up the facade on satellite radios that nothing had changed. It was a dangerous dance. Eleven men in Ryan's Delta Force unit knew this all too well as they moved out in camouflaged yachts. Extracting a nuclear warhead from the clutches of madmen was like removing a bullet lodged in someone's spine. One false move and it was all over. The key was to get to it before it was set in place.

Ryan waited until one by one his men called in to the primary operations vessel, signaling that they'd successfully boarded the five other ships, subdued the crews, and had the torpedoes in U.S. possession. Thomas Wims, portable tracking systems analyst, gave the signal. GPS buoys were in place. Underwater GPS was locked and loaded.

As the last call came in Ryan looked at Lieutenants Ken Christopher and Ethan Adams, fast friends as well as damned good soldiers who'd always had his back. Each man knew his role and said nothing, simply put in his breathing apparatus and lowered his scuba mask over his eyes before taking a backward plunge into the jewel-blue sea.

Underwater silence enveloped them, leaving each man to listen to his own breathing and the thud of his heartbeat in his ears.

The first order of business was to take out the underwater stabilization crew. There would be men waiting below the enemy vessel's hull to guide the nuclear warhead that was being lowered by ship crane into the correct position within the crater. Those men had to be neutralized without blood being let. Sharks weren't the worst of the possible threat; it was the potential of the enemy surface team seeing a plume of crimson crest the water.

Yet the silence provided cover; so did the enemy dive team's lack of communication back to their own vessel. According to the professor, there would be no headset radio contact. The nervous enemy crew wanted no excess transmissions on the day of the mission that could possibly be detected by U.S. forces. Ryan swam directly at the three men, making hand gestures toward the surface and flashing a handheld tracking unit. As expected, the nervous enemy dive team waited for Ryan and the men who flanked him to come in close, clearly worried that something on the surface had gone wrong. It had.

With the flash strike of cobra-like training, breathing apparatus was cut; flailing arms and legs were overpowered. Four minutes is a long time to hold a drowning man. Hooks tethered lifeless bodies to rocky cavern graves. Ryan signaled up with a strong thumb pointing to the surface. It was time to take the ship.

Georgetown, Washington, DC . . .

Mia walked up three long flights to her tiny one-bedroom apartment. Max, her gunmetal-gray kitten, greeted her at the door by pouncing on her feet and making her laugh when she almost dropped the mail.

"Okay, okay, you bad little boy, I missed you, too." She tried to pet him and he playfully swiped at her hand and then darted away to claim the windowsill. "Just like all the men in my life—a pain in my ass and rude. But you always come back to Momma when you want something, don't you."

Moving to the kitchen counter after depositing her mail on the coffee table, setting her briefcase on the floor, and dropping her coat on the sofa, she rummaged in the cabinets for Max's food.

"I could've left you in the shelter, you know—and it wasn't my fault that they had a policy of fixing you rescue-type guys before we were allowed to adopt you. One day you'll thank me," she added, putting a pouch of dried food in his bowl and freshening his water. "And you behave for my girl Camille while I'm gone. No trying to run out on M Street or hissing at her."

Mia stooped down and stroked Max's chin as he rubbed himself against her legs and finally submitted to the attention he'd sought all along. His loud purr intensified as her hand flowed over his back and he arched against her palm.

"Typical," she murmured with a smile and then

set down his food for him. "It's all about what's in it for you. But I love you anyway."

After quickly washing her hands, Mia stared at the dismal choices in her fridge and then grabbed a plastic bag to begin tossing out everything she knew would spoil while she was away for the week. Giving her presentation out loud every night without the benefit of her PowerPoint slides had been something she'd practiced for nearly a month. Picking up out loud where her mind left off, she recited the facts to Max—who was eagerly grazing and ignoring her—trying to make them seem interesting as she played with different voice inflections to create verbal emphasis.

"Haiti, seven-point-zero . . . Chile, eight-point-eight, with Okinawa, Japan, experiencing a seven-point-oh quake the same day. Then Baja California's, which stretched to Nevada and Mexico at a seven-point-two on the Richter scale, with another that hit Southern California at six-point-six, and most recently northern Indonesia—Sumatra—at seven-point-seven. And now New Zealand. With Chile's quake alone, the earth as you are well aware shifted three whole inches off its axis, time reversed by milliseconds, and the city of impact moved by ten feet. Colleagues, this is what is taking place naturally. But the question is, what would happen if this already sped-up natural process were given assistance via man-made intervention?"

Mia paused for dramatic effect, holding the

garbage bag out as though surveying an invisible audience. "Currently, our major metropolitan areas are struggling with ways to keep civilian populations safe in conventional terms. But as a part of our practical, applied research, we must ask ourselves whether we can prevent the use of natural disasters as a new part of global warfare. These sites must be guarded no less than our major railways, airlines, tunnels, and national monuments."

Walking and talking out loud, Mia gathered up the trash, tied it with a twist-tie, and headed for the garbage chute, murmuring her presentation to herself.

"The very site of this conference, Manhattan, New York, sits on fault lines that run from the Flatiron District to Clason Point along FDR Drive, from midpoint in the East River up to Randall's Island Park on the other side of the Triborough Bridge. There's another that goes from New York Route 9A on the bank of the Hudson River, through Central Park, and through the East River to Hunter's Point. Another runs all the way from Route 46 near Fort Lee in New Jersey in a straight line to Roosevelt Island, crossing both the Hudson and East Rivers, with yet another fault traversing the Harlem River Drive and the Major Deegan Expressway. Finally, and not including the one beneath Staten Island, one of the longest-running fault lines stretches from western New York, through the Flatiron District, across two rivers, and terminates on the other side of the Brooklyn-Queens Expressway and the Williamsburg Bridge."

Satisfied, she nodded and closed the trash chute, then walked back to her open apartment door before Max could look up from his food and escape.

"If any of these faults were to be compromised by either an act of aggression or by natural disaster, bridges, major tunnels like the Lincoln Tunnel, highways, and densely populated real estate could all contribute to a disaster that makes what happened in Haiti seem minimal."

Mia closed her eyes for a moment as she locked her apartment door, seeing the brightly colored slides in her mind's eye. "According to models run by both the U.S. Geological Survey and IRIS—Incorporated Research Institutions for Seismology—along with the New Mexico Tech Instrument Center's Program for Array Seismic Studies of the Continental Lithosphere, a seven-point-zero in Manhattan would look like this. An eight-point-eight would look like this."

Warm fur against her pant legs and a loud purr for attention jolted Mia out of her mental practice. "Pretty macabre stuff, isn't it, boy?" she said, giving the feline a quick pet on the head. "Lemme wash my hands and then you can climb in my lap." She ignored the text chime on her BlackBerry, already knowing who it was. "No, Josh," she said, shaking her head and turning on the hot water. "You cannot come over. Go away!"

When Max looked up at her with a confused,

forlorn expression, she scooped him up and nuzzled him. "Oh, baby, not you. Just Josh."

Rewarded by a gentle return nuzzle, she carried Max with her into the bedroom and deposited him on his favorite spot on her overstuffed chair amid the pillows. Mia looked around. Truly, there was nothing to do but go get some dinner, call Camille, rehearse one more time, and then go to bed early. The sad fact was, because this was her life, and not having a social one to speak of, she'd overplanned; she hadn't left herself anything to do the night before the big conference except worry.

She'd been packed for three days, her suitcase waiting all ready in her bedroom the way an expectant mother would wait to dash off to a maternity ward. Her outfit for the morning commute to New York by Amtrak was pressed and ready. It was the tan suit with cream silk tank top, pearls, and neutral hose, black low-heeled Nine West pumps that said *Serious, staid, and professional.* So predictable.

Mia let out a long sigh and scratched Max's favorite spot beneath his chin.

Fort Bragg, North Carolina . . .

Ryan exited the C-140 with his men. Muscle fatigue, cuts, bruises, and sleep deprivation haunted his body, tearing at his tendons and ligaments to the point where even blinking hurt. But after the kill-or-be-killed mission he'd just survived, hurting was good. He was glad to be alive.

The battalion commander, Lieutenant Colonel Andrew Mitchell, also affectionately known by the troops as "the old man," greeted them on the tarmac with a solid salute, unspoken pride lifting his barrel chest.

As the commander snapped his arm out of the salute, his focus landed on Ryan. "I don't have to tell men of your caliber job well done, Captain—but I'm going to say it anyway. Gentlemen, job well done."

"Thank you, sir," Ryan replied, relief and a sense of accomplishment sweeping through him as he spoke. "Just doing our jobs, sir."

Colonel Mitchell nodded, but he held each man's gaze with appreciation for a moment as skilled ground crews began unloading the hazardous cargo from the belly of the C-140. It didn't have to be said. These men had done more than their jobs; they had averted a catastrophe.

"Captain Ryan, follow me to my office. Your men can temporarily stand down."

"Yes, sir," Ryan replied, and then briefly turned to his men before following the colonel. "As you were."

It was a short walk to the waiting jeep, and Ryan felt every death match he'd had with an enemy combatant as he climbed into the vehicle next to Colonel Mitchell. The pair rode in chauffeured silence, only briefly acknowledging the colonel's staff as they entered his office.

"At ease, Captain," Colonel Mitchell said in a weary tone. "You probably need some R and R. I hate to say it, but that's not going to happen right away."

Ryan took a seat adjacent the colonel's desk after the commander sat down. He said nothing, just watched the colonel's expression as he flipped though a report then returned his gaze to Ryan.

"Tomorrow morning, the Global Earthquake and Volcanic Activity Conference in New York City will convene, bringing together some of the most brilliant minds of the twenty-first century," Mitchell said flatly. "Under normal circumstances, this summit would be the jurisdiction of the feds to protect, and the FBI would be all over our asses about a jurisdictional boundary breech, citing the Posse Comitatus Act, if we sent Delta Force in there. But given what just went down in the Azores, the POTUS views protecting these national and international minds as a matter of national security—and gave us the sign-off due to the fact that we are still in hot pursuit of the masterminds of the Azores plot."

Ryan nodded. "Understood, sir."

CHAPTER 3

The shrill bleat of the alarm clock jolted Mia awake, but it didn't make her immediately open her eyes. Five A.M. already? Sheesh . . .

It felt as though her inner lids were lined by a fine grade of sandpaper, and it seemed like she'd only just drifted off to sleep a few moments ago. But the fitful tangle of covers between her legs, and the fact that Max had abandoned her to seek peace among the chair pillows instead of draping himself across her head the way he normally did, told her that she'd tossed and turned all night.

Slowly dragging her body to the edge of the bed, she met the early morning with a mixture of surly disdain and then sudden dread. *This morning I have to catch a train.*

Stark reality propelled her from the tangle of sheets like a shot. Max just gazed up at her for a moment and gave her the evil eye, then hunkered back down into his warm spot with the air of silent belligerence that only a feline can serve.

Half stumbling to the bathroom, she quickly dispensed with her morning routine, then showered and hurriedly dressed, all the while feeling the anxiety snake through her. Max didn't even eye her as she made her bed. They both shared that—he wasn't a morning person, either. There wasn't time for coffee; Starbucks awaited in the train station. But as she stared in the mirror through her tortoiseshell glasses and applied a last dab of lip gloss, Mia sighed. Contact lenses were out this morning. She'd have to pack them. The lack of sleep and spring allergies had left her eyes puffy and irritated. Forget looking cute on the train or possibly at the conference. But what did that matter anyway?

The glasses made her look more serious . . . smarter, maybe even a bit older, she told herself as she glimpsed her reflection one last time. That had to be a good thing, given the conference attendees who were sure to be there. Yes. That was the look she wanted, that of a very serious individual who knew her stuff. Especially if David might be there. God help her.

Shoving her contacts and solution into her purse, she glanced around her apartment one last time and then went to stroke Max, who at that hour could not have cared less.

"You behave yourself, all right? Ignore me if

you want, buster. But remember, I could have gone for a puppy when I fell in love with you," she murmured and then gave Max an affectionate stroke beneath the chin. "I'll be back soon."

Max's response was a very lazy stretch and a constant purr. But he didn't bother following her to the door.

Finally a chime on her cell phone let her know the cab she'd arranged for last night was downstairs waiting for her on the street. No Metro today—not with a suitcase, laptop, purse, et al. With her luck she would have snagged a huge run in her stockings trying to lug her bags up and down the subway steps.

"Coming right down," she told the cabbie.

She pretended not to be annoyed as she bumped her bags down the brownstone apartment building's front steps and the cabdriver simply watched her. The guy could have at least gotten out when he popped the hood, she thought as she struggled to get the roller bag over the lip of the trunk. He had the same light caramel coloring as her ex-fiancé, and similar features that made both their ethnicities hard to judge at a glance. They also shared the same haughty air of indifference, and this cabbie acted as though grabbing a bag were beneath him somehow.

Dr. David Williams would have behaved no differently, Mia thought as she finally got momentum to work with her and she released the bag with a thud that rocked the vehicle. Only this guy's almond-shaped eyes were dark brown and David's were a lighter pecan tone. Both had close-cropped hair that gave way to natural waves. From her last dealings with David she knew she'd forever be prejudiced against so-called pretty boys. This just reminded her why.

Determined not to stress over all the little things that could go wrong at the conference or had already ticked her off this morning, Mia finally settled into the back of the cab and braced herself for a return to the city. She fastened her gaze to the light traffic they passed along the way, saying a quiet prayer that David wouldn't be at this event, but was already pretty sure he would be. Like Columbia University's entire geophysicist community wouldn't attend. Right.

Okay, so seeing him there would be awkward, but not devastating. She could take refuge in the fact that she'd been the one to break things off; he'd been the one to act ugly as a result. But neither of them would risk career embarrassment by being other than civil in public. They were both adults. Intellectuals, even. That was the mantra she'd kept repeating inside her head the moment she'd learned that she'd be presenting.

But the other half of her anxiety was family-related. Funny thing was, she'd just admitted that to herself as the train station came into view. Since she'd had a silent cabbie, one not trying to make small talk in the morning, it allowed her brain to seize upon every worry she owned.

The simple truth was that she'd find time during the weekend following the conference to visit her now widowed mother, as well as a host of friends and cousins from the old neighborhood . . . and therefore would have to field the number one question they had about her life: What happened to that guy she was going to marry?

Mia listened to the cabbie's monotonous announcement of the fare and gave him back exact change. They stared at each other for a moment.

"You have a *nice* day," the young man said with attitude and a slight, indistinguishable accent.

Mia then peeled off two singles and held them out to him, watching his scowling expression improve. "I would have gladly given you more, but ask yourself, did you earn it? Thanks for the help with the bags, by the way."

He took her money without comment and simply popped the hood. Man, she hated young cabdrivers. No chivalry like the older dudes. Shaking off her slight annoyance, she walked from the cab with purpose, then dug in her raincoat pocket to drop a single bill in a homeless guy's hand.

"You gonna be blessed, miss," the homeless man yelled after her as she walked forward without breaking stride.

"You have a nice day, too," she replied by rote, but somehow meaning it. She glanced at him over her shoulder and offered him a smile.

The man beamed at her with a brownish yellow snaggle-toothed grin and pointed at her with a dirty forefinger that poked out through his ragged gloves. "I'ma remember you. Yep. LeRoy never forgets a kind turn. Gonna make sure Jesus got you covered. Bless you, purty lady."

Mia nodded and picked up her pace. Growing up in New York had taught her that if she lingered more than three to five seconds, she'd either hear a long life story that she really didn't want to know—or get her purse snatched. Where she came from, there were eight million stories in the naked city.

Disappearing beneath the huge, arched doorways of Union Station, she was now in the safety zone: Vagrants weren't allowed to cross the capital city's pristine marble floors or to hang out in front of its overpriced, gleaming, brass-appointed shops. Even at this hour of the morning, commuters were already making demands at coffee-and-doughnut watering holes. Once she'd collected her ticket from an electronic kiosk, she headed for the strongest coffee scent that was closest to her gate.

When she got in line, she chuckled quietly to herself. Dr. Cortland had beaten her to the punch and was several people ahead of her. Once he'd paid and stepped to the side, she gave him a little wave when he looked up from managing his change.

With a broad smile, he came over to give her a good-natured hug. "I see you've packed like my wife used to. Forty percent shoes, yes?"

Mia laughed. "How did you know? But I do have the excuse that I'll be staying through the weekend to visit family, and who knows what they'll want to do."

"I don't pretend to understand more than that the handbag must somehow and very oddly match the shoes—and perish the thought that the same shoes might be worn twice. This I learned after fifty-three years of marriage and travel with the great love of my life."

"I'm not that bad," Mia said as he strode away to collect his coffee.

"Mine is not to reason why, mine is but to do or die—I believe some very famous wise man once said." He gave her a little bow as he took a sip from his cup and stood beside her in line, as though escorting her to the counter.

Being near Dr. Cortland this morning suddenly made her miss her dad. It was always a fleeting discovery that flowed through her quickly and then was gone. Even though their brand of humor was slightly different, her father and her mentor were, as old folks said, cut from the same cloth. And she'd also heard the wistfulness in Dr. Cortland's tone when speaking of his dead wife, Mildred. It was that same genial remembrance that her mother owned when speaking of her father, one that was always a tad bittersweet even while laughing.

As Mia stepped up to the counter she couldn't imagine having the constancy of someone to love, dote on, care about, and fight with for more than half a century—but also knowing that you'd make up with them when you did disagree. Mia stifled a yawn as she placed her order, wondering how her grandparents' generation was able to do that through world wars, segregation, even the Depression. Yet they'd held it together.

"You were up all night, be honest," Dr. Cortland said, admonishing her as she stepped aside to wait for her order.

"Huh? Oh, yeah . . . ," Mia replied after lurching away from her private thoughts. "Didn't sleep a wink."

"You should close your eyes on the train and stop overstudying," he said, following her to the pickup station. "This first day is light fare. We check in and then register for the conference, attend the obligatory welcoming lunch, and if you feel so inclined, you can sit through the boring organizational update panels where all the sponsors get to toot their horns. But me, I will be taking a nap." He leaned in and gave her a toothy grin. "That is the secret of my youth. I have learned to pace myself in accordance to the European model. I take my time eating and digesting my food. I walk lots every day. But I nap and then have a burst of energy. Then early to bed and early to rise."

He snapped his arthritic fingers to make a point. "And I turn off all worries with my nightstand light to sleep like a baby. I set my mind to worry about it tomorrow."

"Were it only that easy," she said, collecting her latte. "But I'll remember that. It sure would've helped me get up this morning."

"I had a dear colleague who was Caribbean-born. Dr. Winslow. He used to say, 'Ian, you get up before the cock put on 'im drawers. You keep that good habit going and my grandmother will mistake you for one of her own children.' When you get a few gray hairs you'll learn not to sweat the small stuff, and then one day you'll figure out that it's all small stuff . . . that's when you'll go to bed early and will wake up before the rooster crows—or puts on his drawers, as the case may be."

Mia just nodded as she added two packs of raw sugar to her latte. She needed that pep talk, and it was one of the things she loved so dearly about Dr. Cortland—he was an extremely brilliant man, but also funny and down-to-earth. He wore his genius in an everyday man's clothes and didn't browbeat everyone around him about how smart he was. That kind of humility was rare in the circles she traveled in, where education and intellect were the currency, and the snobbery that went along almost expected.

They wheeled their bags to the gate side by side in companionable silence—his bag dwarfed by hers in both size and weight. He had a *Washington Post* under his arm that she could tell he was itching to open. But he needed a place to sit down and wait. She scanned the seating area and could feel her blood pressure rising as traveling students and businesspeople sprawled out over the seats while an eighty-six-year-old man stood quietly, patiently, sipping his coffee.

She knew that he'd be mortified if she intervened in his behalf, but the New Yorker in her could only take it for a few moments before she found herself moving forward. To spare her mentor's dignity, she'd get them both a seat and do it in a way that seemed as though she was the one who needed to sit down.

"Oh, Doctor, here's a coupla seats," she announced loudly, walking up to a sleeping student and promptly moving his bag to the floor where it belonged. She let it hit the floor with a loud, challenging thud. The relocation freed up three seats. She motioned toward his sneakers, which would have dirtied her raincoat, when he glared at her. "Excuse me."

The student sat up and frowned. Mia gave him the death-ray grit. Everything in her body language challenged the kid, who looked like he was about to protest for a moment. Mia gave him a sidelong glance that said, *Don't start none, won't be none.*

The professor just opened his paper with a very quiet chuckle and enjoyed another sip of his coffee. Interestingly enough, several other students took their feet off the seats and moved their luggage to the floor so that other passengers could finally sit down.

Yeah . . . maybe what David had said was true—you could take the girl out of Harlem but you sure couldn't take Harlem out of the girl.

CHAPTER 4

New York City . . .

A solid night's sleep, a hot shower, a good shave, and a visit to the base barbershop, along with a handful of Motrin, made him feel considerably better. Ryan glimpsed himself in the reflective glass as he walked through LaGuardia International Airport.

Yeah, he could pass for a conference attendee. A military flight had gotten him to New York City from Fort Bragg, North Carolina, without the formality of checking his weapons. But now with a laptop slung over one shoulder and towing a very heavy suitcase, and having ditched his Brazilian biker image, he definitely looked like a clean-cut Ivy League professor. Black designer nonprescription lenses, brown tweed jacket with suede elbow patches, tan Dockers, and penny loafers worked to help him blend in.

"The Marriott downtown—85 West Street," he told the cabdriver once his turn came up in the taxi stand line, and then he began reading messages on his encrypted BlackBerry.

Faces of terrorist operatives who had been involved in the Azores plot scrolled beneath his thumbnail prompt. He would remember those faces and soon delete them from his cell phone. Every dossier was already committed to memory. Now all he had to do was check into the hotel, then there'd be enough time to do a recon around the building, and then he'd slide in and out of various sessions, keeping his focus on those professors most likely to be targeted for kidnapping.

A text from his unit's second in command let him know that both Ethan and Ken were in place. FBI and CIA would also be crawling all over the building with local plainclothes law enforcement, now that everyone was aware of the way in which the world's greatest minds could be used against their will and against humanity. This time, no one from Homeland Security would be asleep at the wheel. At least not in the Big Apple. A coordinated effort was the only way to make sure of that.

Ryan stared out the window as his cab crept through traffic toward the Financial District. Even after all these years it still blew his mind that the towers of the World Trade Center were gone. For a moment he looked away, training his line of vision on the traffic ahead of them and feeling the muscle in his jaw pulse.

"It's a crying shame, ain't it?" the cabbie said, revealing a thick, Italian-by-way-of-Queens accent and glancing up to look at Ryan in his rearview mirror.

"Yeah. The bullshit still gets to me," Ryan admitted, carefully assessing the cabbie.

"Pisses me off, too, ya know," the cabbie replied, leaning back to watch the road and also to give Ryan more attention than was probably safe. He threw a meaty arm across the seat, and the fleshy appendage stuck to the bulletproof Plexiglas that separated them. "I don't think we're ever gonna get over it, even if they build the monument and what have ya. You're right. It was pure bullshit. But me . . . I'm just praying that it never happens again."

"You and me both," Ryan said, handing the man the fare as he opened the door. "But I'm ready to do a little more than pray about it, if they come for us again." When the cabbie gave him a wide grin, Ryan issued him a thumbs-up. "Keep the change."

A gracious Marriott hotel doorman greeted Ryan and immediately took his bags. "Staying with us for the conference, sir? May I bring these to hotel registration?"

"Yes, thank you," Ryan said, remembering to be easy and to allow the hotel employee to handle what was probably enough artillery to stop a small army. Aside from a few workout clothes, sneakers, some underwear, and a couple of suit changes to be presentable at the functions, everything else was urban warfare equalizers and hollow-points.

Under normal circumstances, standing in the interminably long check-in line would have gotten on his nerves. But this was the perfect opportunity to peruse the incoming guests, to see which professors on his target-of-value list to protect were here and who they'd come with. One of his main PhDs to keep an eye on was just two people from the check-in desk. Dr. Ian Cortland had an extensive and impressive dossier in the area of seismic geology and volcanic research. But he was also widowed with a son who had perished young in an auto accident, Ryan noted. If he was abducted and tortured, at his age, he might well suffer a heart attack—but what could they use against him to leverage the old man? His circumstances were very different than the younger Dr. Patel's had been.

Ryan inconspicuously sent his gaze around the lobby. Dr. William Albright—London. Dr. Zubair Molefi—Ghana. Dr. James Lee—China. Those professors talking with Dr. Cortland definitely made up an international brain trust, and that wasn't counting the lesser mental stars in line. The four lead academics represented probably two hundred years' worth of brain talent and were an invaluable international treasure. Pulling out his cell phone,

Ryan quickly sent his unit a text to let them know he'd already spotted four of the foremost authorities in the subject matters that could be used by disaster terrorists.

However, their so-called idle banter was enough to make him glaze over. Although he'd taken *rocks for jocks,* as his major was nicknamed up at West Point, these old guys took intellectual sparring to an entirely different level. Ryan smiled to himself as he watched them interact. Maybe this was a job for the guys in Area 51, because they sure sounded like aliens to him.

But then something happened that he wasn't prepared for . . . something so unexpected and so bizarre that for a moment he was paralyzed where he stood. He had seen her name on the attendee list when he was briefed for the mission and pushed that knowledge way down deep in his psyche. But there was no repressing how he felt the moment he saw her. There wasn't enough military training to keep his pulse from kicking up a notch, even if he was able to maintain a deadpan expression.

She floated off the elevators with a stack of blue folders in her arms and walked up to the bevy of old men waiting in line. Her voice had already been permanently etched into his soul, just like her easy smile and casual gait that was as sexy as hell. She didn't even see him; she was focused on her mission to pass out folders. God, she looked fantastic.

The years had matured her in a way that made him know she was all woman now. Outrageously long-legged and beautiful. Gone was the young girl. She carried herself with an air of confidence. Mia was in command. She wore no ring, and her tone with the men around her appeared to be professionally engaging. Unable to do otherwise, he hung on her every word, mesmerized.

"Teamwork pays off, gentlemen," she said, giving Dr. Cortland his folder and then passing out the others to his colleagues.

"Do you see why she is my favorite research fellow?" Dr. Cortland replied, gallantly kissing the back of Mia's hand. "Brilliant with savvy enough to navigate the system so we old codgers don't have to go through the dreary rigmarole of standing in a registration line after this interminable wait in the lobby."

"My dear, you are a godsend, as generous as you are lovely. Thank you," Dr. Albright said with a smile. "Ian, now we understand why you refuse to retire."

"You'd better watch out," Dr. Lee said, chuckling. "We could ruin détente by stealing Dr. Austin away from you."

"Ah, but not before we put in a bid for her at our university," Dr. Molefi said, causing the small group of men to both agree and deepen their laughter.

"I wouldn't hear of it," Dr. Cortland said, waving them off with a wider smile. "Her plan was flawless. The timing impeccable. Just as we are nearing the check-in desk, she has returned with our folders, badges, itineraries, and programs." He turned to Mia and bowed. "We are in your debt, and please do not think we are in any way trying to take advantage." He brought a finger to his lips. "In some circles it might be seen as a feminist affront."

"No worries," Mia said, her beautiful, lilting laughter flowing over the crowd to reach Ryan's insides. "You held my space in line, so we're even."

"Touché!" Dr. Cortland announced and then stepped up to the front desk.

Ryan took in a slow inhale and released it with careful deliberation. Dr. Austin . . . wow. She'd reached her goal and was obviously doing well. Quiet pride filled him on the next inhale. But this was also a dangerous scenario that could possibly blow his cover.

He could get out of the line now and possibly make his way to a men's room to wait until she was gone. But that was also a risky proposition. What if she saw him bolt? She'd have questions; it would raise her suspicions. Then again, maybe she would see him, briefly acknowledge him, and not want to make small talk . . . after all, theirs was a relationship gone awry. But Mia wasn't like that. At least she never came across as a woman to hold a grudge.

Regardless, this had the potential to be both a blessing and a disaster. She was the only one here who knew he'd been in the military. She was also

obviously on the in with many of the men he needed
to guard, which meant he could get closer to them
than he'd imagined without raising any suspicions.

Caught in an untenable position, he decided to
hold his ground and sent a text to his unit. It was
simple and killed two birds with one stone: *Fnd
way in thru old contct. U stay on trgts 2-4, lemme
take 1.*

But it was a very spurious plan. Mia could
also accidentally make a remark that tipped off a
yet-unknown predator who was possibly here doing reconnaissance. If the subject of his military
career came up, he'd have to quickly diffuse it. Just
like he'd have to quickly diffuse the way she was
making him feel.

With her room key in hand and the professors beginning to fan out toward the elevators, she turned
around and looked up at the line that had been behind her—then froze. It all happened in slow motion. He was standing there looking more handsome
than he had ten years prior. He now wore glasses
and looked so disarmingly fantastic in them and in
his tweed jacket . . . his shoulders filled out the
simple garment in a way that seemed illegal. Without warning, butterflies took flight within her belly.
It made no sense, and she had no right to even feel
that way, but there was no helping it. He was looking down at his cell phone and obviously hadn't

seen her. She searched his hands. No sign of a ring. But that was foolish, and it didn't mean anything, anyway. She looked at his luggage, which seemed all male, praying that no lucky woman would soon sidle up to him with her roll-on.

"Uhmmm . . . excuse me," Mia said to Dr. Cortland, who was engaged in lively debate. "We'll meet up at the luncheon?"

"To be sure," he said, not missing a beat as he got on the elevator. "We'll reconvene and continue this argument in a few hours."

The elderly gentlemen around her chuckled and piled onto the waiting car. She backed off and slowly walked toward the source of her distraction, all the while trying to come up with a way to say something as simple as hello.

"Ryan?" she said as calmly as possible once she'd moved in close to him.

He looked up and smiled. She held her breath, remembering that megawatt flash of stark white against smooth brown skin.

"Mia? Wow . . ."

She needed smelling salts.

"I didn't know you were coming to this conference," she stammered. "I thought you were—"

"Yeah, I changed careers," he said, cutting her off. "How's the family . . . your Mom and Dad?"

She looked down. "Lost Dad a few years ago, but Mom is getting better with that."

"Oh, hey . . . I'm really, really sorry," he said in an awkward tone, shoving his phone into his pocket.

For a moment he stepped forward as though to hug her and then seemed to think better of it. She was glad he did, because she would have probably passed out.

"It's cool," she said, now the one sounding awkward. "He was sick—prostate cancer . . . and wouldn't go to the doctor. You know how that generation is about things like that."

"I would have come to the funeral, had I known. I'm sorry I didn't know . . . please let your Mom know that for me."

"I will. That would mean a lot to her to hear that. I'll see her this weekend. You know you can't come home to the city and not go do the rounds with the folks. Good thing my sister is still in Houston with the kids, or she'd be plying me with margaritas and insisting on back-to-back ladies' nights. Then we'd have to go get my brother's wife down in Jersey, or she'd be offended and whatever. Family drama hasn't changed. Just got more people added to it."

He laughed, nodding, the rich, deep timber of his voice liquefying her bones as much as it dissolved the awkwardness between them.

"I'm in hiding," he said, placing a finger to his lips. "Promise you won't out me and tell any of my peeps I'm here. This is an in-and-out mission."

She laughed and shook her head. "Your secret is

safe with me . . . I wish I had thought ahead that far and had come up with a cover." She shrugged, loving the easy way their conversation just fell into place again after all the years that had gone by. "So, tell me—where are you now?"

"NYU," he said, thinking fast on his feet, remembering the ruse he had prepared. "I was gonna ask you the same."

"Oh, my God, Ryan . . . NYU? Wow . . . that means you're local. I know your mom must be in seventh heaven!"

"And in my business," he said, trying to get the excited timbre of her voice out of his bloodstream before she gave him wood. "But enough about me . . . where are you?"

"In DC at the Smithsonian . . . broke, living in a third-floor walk-up in Georgetown on a postdoctoral research fellowship—what can I say?"

He could feel his voice drop despite his attempts to keep things light. "I'm really proud of you, Mia. That's awesome."

She blushed and that almost made him reach out and touch her cheek. His fingers burned to stroke the satiny soft skin that seemed to glow from an inner light she possessed. Then she offered him a little self-deprecating shrug.

"It's long hours, no money, and lots of data," she said with a small laugh, telling him everything in the nothing statement.

"It's important, a real accomplishment, and I'm

jealous of the guy who gets to wait up for you after those long hours." He waited, wanting clarity, even if it did cross a professional line.

She studied the floor but her smile widened. He wanted to punch himself—what the hell had possessed him to kick a corny line like that to a woman of Mia's caliber—especially while on a mission?

"No need to be jealous. The only one waiting up for me is Max, my rescue kitten, and even he isn't all that impressed when I get home."

Okay . . . big information download had just happened. He needed to reposition his brain for the fact check. Ryan smiled as a cover for instant distress. A woman this fine was living alone at night and researching by day with a bunch of old geezers whom Viagra couldn't help?

"Yeah . . . well," he said carefully. "I know what you mean. Sometimes people aren't ready for a commitment to a person who has a demanding career."

Mia looked up at him, but her smile had faded. "Yeah . . . well, that about says it all. Glad we got to say hi, though . . . enjoy the conference."

"No, no, no," he said quickly, grabbing her arm and holding it by the elbow as she turned to leave. "That's not what I meant. I wasn't referring to the past. I should have said that it's their loss."

She looked up at him with the biggest, most beautiful brown eyes he'd ever seen. Right there in the lobby, for just a moment, if he could have stopped time he would have removed her glasses and taken her mouth with his. But that was a no-can-do.

"What happened before," he said very slowly, lowering his voice to a private murmur, "was my bad. It was youth and not knowing how to multi-task . . . or how to communicate and prioritize. But what I was really trying to say is, anybody who didn't take you off the market was foolish—especially if he didn't have the mitigating circumstances of time and distance like we did."

His blurted confession brought back a small, trembling smile to her lips. It was the kind of expression that made him not see that there was now a huge gap in the line, and it made him temporarily forget for a few seconds that he had artillery in his suitcase.

"It was both our bad," she said quietly. "No blame."

"Are you going to the lunch?" he said, finally looking up and moving up in the line when the person behind them cleared his throat.

"Yeah . . . but I'll be with my mentor and his colleagues," she said, hesitating. "I'll introduce you to them. Those old men are beyond brilliant and are also nice—not like a lot of others of their caliber that I'm sure you've met."

"Sure, sure," Ryan said, relieved that he could see Mia in the luncheon event room without feeling compelled to sit with her. He had to stay on mission, but damn . . . she was a helluva distraction. And even though she would introduce him and get him in close, the last thing he wanted to do was to get into a probing conversation with academic brainiacs who probably knew everyone. "Let's play lunch by ear, though . . . I don't know who all will be here from NYU. I'm sorta new," he hedged.

"No problem at all. I'm sure your colleagues will be there and, you know, networking. I have to sit with Dr. Cortland and his colleagues during the lunch, because afterward, they're all going to go to their rooms to chill out—saving their energy for the all-day presentations tomorrow."

He nodded, worry gripping his gut. When he'd tossed out the cover lie about his affiliation to NYU, he hadn't thought of the whole networking component. This was a small, insular fraternity. He was gonna have to work on weaving his tale a little better than he had—but he'd worry about that later. Meantime she'd also told him where the men he was monitoring would be. He could put his unit on watching their rooms and could gather more intel on their research and projects from Mia, just to better understand how their work could be used by insurgents. At least that was the very neat justification he gave himself.

"Yeah, we've gotta do what we've gotta do . . . but maybe if there's not a lot going on this afternoon . . . maybe we could walk around the area, see what's new down here, and find somewhere to grab a beer for old times' sake?"

Now he knew he was insane. Take her on a second-pass recon with him? Madness. Then again, if the wrong side was watching whoever was watching the professors, this diversion would make it seem as though he was a decoy and not really a part of anything—especially if any of them thought they recognized him from the Azores meeting with Professor Patel. Now, that made perfect sense.

On the other hand, as he stared at Mia, he also knew that the very wrong side of his brain could have taken over to rationalize the entire thing. In this very moment he wasn't sure if getting closer to a person who was on the in with the top professors was his sole motive, or if his judgment had gotten clouded.

"I'd like that," she finally said, covering a quiet laugh with her hand when the guy behind them cleared his throat again. "Tonight, dinner is on our own, to allow for people with jet lag to get rested and for people to catch up with colleagues during unstructured time."

"Cool . . . ," he said, removing his phone from his pocket again. "You mind?"

She tilted her head, questioning.

"No . . . I'm not taking a call. I wanted to know if I can have your number so I can text you about meeting later to go for a walk."

"Oh," she said, moving up in the line with him

and then carefully repeating her cell phone number. "Okay . . . I'd better go," she added as he got to the front desk.

"All right," he murmured, watching her pivot away from him and head toward the elevators.

He would have gladly waited another hour in line just to stand there in her presence making small talk. She kept her eyes fastened on the elevators, almost seeming as though she was willing it to hurry up and collect her to whisk her away from him. Could he blame her? But she'd told him so much in such a short time. And out of duty, he'd lied to the woman—a decent, honorable woman who deserved nothing but the truth. Yet that duty didn't stop him from wanting her or needing her, nor did it keep him from trying to figure out a way to repair the past.

This was so not a part of his deployment orders.

CHAPTER 5

Mia shut the hotel room door behind her and leaned against it with her eyes closed for a moment. Dear God in heaven, what was she going to do now?

Her heart was beating so fast that she could barely catch her breath. Her face was warm and her knees weren't knees any longer; they'd turned into some kind of wobbly confection. Oh . . . my . . . God. Ryan Mason was in the building, at the conference, and looked good enough to literally eat.

She fanned her face with her hands and then pushed off the door, wishing she'd worn her contacts this morning, wishing that she'd said something witty, wishing she'd worn a less plain suit—but then again, what would have been appropriate?

Gathering up her purse and laptop from the floor, she moved them to the long Internet-accessible desk and then came back to collect her suitcase.

Rolling it to the closet, she pulled out the folding valet, then lifted her luggage to sit atop and opened it to begin hanging up her clothes.

Did she change for lunch or would that be too obvious? Yeah, too obvious. It would be better to change into jeans and sneakers or flats for the walk later. But did she try to put in her contacts now or later? Maybe at the banquet tomorrow . . . stay casual, appear as though this chance meeting was nice but no big deal. Mia held up her plain peach nightgown and then dropped it back into her suitcase with a frown.

"Do not even go there," she told herself firmly and then hung up the rest of her clothes, leaving her lingerie in her luggage and then closing her suitcase before stashing everything behind the closet door.

"That was a long time ago," she muttered to herself as she walked to the large, white-tiled bathroom and stashed her toiletries on the wide marble sink.

For a moment she stopped and smelled the soap, pleased that the Marriott had her favorite Bath & Body Works citrus-ginger soaps and lotions. She glanced at the double-wide tub and how the shower curtain was designed to bow out to make room for more than one person, and then quickly hurried out of the suddenly too-small space.

"Get your mind out of the gutter," she said out loud, beginning to set up her laptop computer. "You don't even really know this man now—a lot can happen to people over time, a lot can change, and you certainly aren't sleeping with him at a career-maker conference!" Mia looked up into the long mirror that faced her above the desk, ignoring the huge king-size bed in the reflection behind her that was covered in a thick white-on-white duvet and fluffy pillows. "Nope. You have *some* pride. You have a career. You have a reputation, Dr. Austin. Remember that."

Mia kicked out of her shoes and stood in front of the mirror in her stocking feet, assessing her face. After a moment she unpinned her severe bun and allowed her hair to fall to her shoulders. It had been six months since anyone, except old man Jackson who worked security, had told her she was pretty—and even he did so in a very discreet and respectful way. When she really thought about it, maybe it had been longer than that.

David was never big on compliments or random displays of affection. After the nasty breakup, where he'd really told her what he'd always thought of her lack of familial pedigree, she hadn't been ready to go out to clubs or to attend the DC-area singles meet-and-greets like her friends had suggested. Just one night of mate-search drama on the Internet had made her take down her online dating profile and go into virtual cyber-hiding. Her nerves were still too raw.

Suddenly every flaw David had seen in her came

to bear on her confidence. Yes . . . she still struggled a little with perfect diction, with overcoming the native New-York-by-way-of-Harlem homegirl patois that would escape when she was relaxed and around friends. He'd teased her relentlessly about "sounding ghetto" when she'd use a little slang in his presence—albeit she never slipped into the comfort of old neighborhood speech patterns while at work or out in public. That had only happened once, a slip around his DC socialite friends.

The rebuff was immediate and stinging as he'd laughed at her phraseology and asked them to forgive his "ghetto girl," then went on to insist she tell them how to say other key words and phrases in New Yorker.

David had opened her up to their bourgeois disdain of anyone perceived not to be from their elite economic station. Then he'd thrown her under the bus before them. She vividly recalled the deep satisfaction that seemed to glitter in his eyes as they'd quickly descended upon her as a curiosity. It was as though he was punishing her for the slip-up, for the mistake of ever daring to embarrass him before his peers. The goal seemed to be to drive home the point to her to never let such a social faux pas happen again.

And as though they'd waited beyond their endurance for the opportunity to chastise an outsider, the women in the group made it their business to let her know just how much of an outsider she was, while the men sipped wine and watched it all from amused spectators' positions.

She'd hated David for that. In a subtly malevolent frenzy of polite conversation his friends had asked her so-called cultural questions with eager smiles, acting as though she were from some foreign land or certainly from some strange reality beyond their grasp, asking about her mother's Puerto Rican heritage and her father's unspectacular African American roots . . . about gangs and crime and all things associated with poverty. All done with smiles, glasses of Merlot and Chardonnay in hands, all done so civilly and with such happy banter that had she taken offense and stepped to any one of them for their rude social ignorance, she would have been what David had claimed: his ghetto girl.

Mia wrapped her arms around herself and closed her eyes for a moment. She'd almost left him that night. It was so humiliating, and yet he saw nothing wrong with it and professed innocence. A couple of years later she'd come to learn that he did know what he was doing by diminishing her. It was simply his method of control—making her feel smaller in every aspect of her being.

Mia slowly opened her eyes and touched the tiny pearl earrings she wore, remembering the day he'd told her that her gold hoops, although small and tasteful, just didn't give her image the polish

it required. She also remembered the day he'd crit-
icized her clothes and then realized how her color
choices had slowly migrated away from the vibrant
realm of reds and royal blues and bold oranges and
living greens and into the realm of tans and grays
and camels and black.

Staring at herself, she swallowed hard. How had
an intelligent woman allowed something like this
to happen? David's influence was a slow, insidious
drip of disapproval that wore away at who she was,
level by level of selfhood, like beach erosion. Until
one day she'd looked up and this was who she'd
become.

Yet it was impossible to lay all the blame at his
feet, because she'd allowed it to happen. He was
older, seemed wiser, had come from an educated
family of means—people who seemed to always
know more than she did; had traveled to places she'd
only dreamed of, had accomplished things that
seemed so far beyond her reach . . . and she so didn't
want to allow her lack of exposure to ultimately reveal her shortcomings. She'd fought all her life to
catch up and learn the things that others had had the
opportunity to be taught just by accident of birth.

But why was lipstick with a little color in it a
bad thing? Who determined what so-called ghetto
was or was not? Why was it wrong to laugh at a
good joke from down deep in your belly? Why was
dancing with your whole body in the groove embarrassing? What made it wrong to wail out loud at

funerals for someone you dearly loved? What was wrong with spicy food cooked with love? What made putting a hand on a hip and telling somebody off a social stigma, especially when they deserved it? What made one mother's brand of tough love worse than another's time-out in a chair? Why should anyone feel ashamed because her parents could only afford rec center dance classes and because during the summer she jumped double Dutch rope in the streets for fun, instead of being given private tennis lessons? Why was she a hot tamale or a whore for emoting out loud when she made love?

Mia quickly turned away from the mirror, and covered her heart with a hand. A mixture of rage at David and complete disappointment at herself made it impossible to meet her own eyes right now. Suddenly the room was too small, too suffocating. She had even allowed the man to take away her spontaneity in bed.

Tears filled her eyes as the full impact of what had happened slammed into her lungs with her next breath. Through small, seemingly innocuous comments, always after David had thoroughly enjoyed himself, her sexuality and sensuality was shredded . . . from the type of music she'd selected to entice him—which was never classical or highbrow enough for a truly cerebral experience; to the dinner she may have prepared to set the mood— which could have been of a finer quality or more gourmet somehow. Then came the morning-after comments. Those were the worst. Death by a thousand tiny cuts.

Those soul-slicing statements delivered between sips of coffee and eggs over easy rang in Mia's head now like a gong. The sarcastic snipes like, "Wow, you certainly enjoyed yourself last night—at least the neighbors can testify to that. They probably thought I had a prostitute in here last night," had initially made her self-consciously laugh and hug him, thinking he was just teasing her.

But soon she realized that, no, he wasn't just verbally jousting with her to rekindle the fire from the night before. He was actually imposing subtle sanctions against her behavior. And although she'd sworn to herself that he could kiss her natural ass and what he said didn't matter, she hadn't been brave enough to just break things off and walk.

Instead, they might argue, where he'd always win by making her feel foolish for challenging him. She'd yell and get emotional; he'd point out how her hysteria made her point moot, and then would decimate her argument by staying calm and seemingly logical, claiming complete ignorance about her charges against him. Sadly, it had taken her two years to actually find her calm voice and say enough is enough.

Shame washed over Mia the more she thought about what she'd allowed. Seeing Ryan again today made the contrast between the men impossible to ignore. It had also made the truth impossible to ignore.

Until now she hadn't admitted to herself that she'd been searching for Ryan Mason's replacement since the day they broke up. After dating serial cheaters for almost a decade and nearly losing hope that she'd find another honorable man, admittedly she had settled into something that felt safe, even if it didn't feel right. That part she couldn't blame on David. He hadn't held her hostage; she could have left the moment she saw his ugly side. But she didn't.

Mia sat down hard on the bed and allowed her head to drop into her hands. A curtain of auburn hair shielded her face from the sun rays that poured through her window. "You are *so stupid*," she whispered as a hot tear ran down the bridge of her nose.

She'd gone for safe, husband material. For all his bullshit, David wasn't going to leave her. He was stable and didn't cheat, was educated, and was gainfully employed without baby-momma drama. He wasn't violent; all he did was snipe and gripe. Well, that was true until they broke up. That's when he'd slapped the taste out of her mouth. One powerful slap had brought her to her senses and made her decision final. But before that had happened, for all his snobbery, she'd believed that David most likely wasn't going to get killed in some foreign land to leave her heart bleeding on a battlefield with him. However, she'd later learned that going for safe had its price, too—the death of her spirit by dishonor.

Mia blinked back tears, sat back, and looked up toward the ceiling, trying to get them to burn away. Truth stabbed into her brain and reminded her of things she hadn't even told her best friend or her sister. Little by little she'd become quieter and quieter, less aggressive and almost mute in bed with David . . . and honestly, guilt had probably allowed her to suffer in silence—because if she were really, really honest, she hadn't been hollering in bed for David anyway. It was an old mental DVD series in her head left over from the nights of Ryan that was the most likely culprit.

Maybe that's why David resented her exuberance so much. Maybe down deep he could sense that his lackluster performance didn't warrant her enthusiasm; who knew? At this juncture, who cared?

But she had to dissect it all in order to finally come to the conclusion that her libido had practically thrashed itself to death in the snare of David's judgment until it had worn itself out. From there, he was totally in control. He'd called the shots and determined when, where, and how they'd made love, when and where they'd go out, whom they would interact with, and *always* how she'd behave.

"Never again," Mia murmured and stood. She wrapped her arms around her waist and took several deep breaths. She hadn't felt the kindle of desire in so long that it didn't make sense. And it took feeling that slow burn to make her realize just how cut off from her own feelings she'd been.

Near nauseous with the full realization of what she'd allowed herself to comply with, Mia turned back to the mirror slowly and then searched for her comb and brush within her purse.

As she redid her bun and touched up her lipstick, then put a little powder on her nose to take away the shine and to rub out the tear streaks, she made a decision: From this day forward she would only live in truth and joy. From this day forward she would only make time for a good person in her life. From this moment on she would not look back to dwell on pain or what shouldn't have been or could have been. No. From this point on she would speak her truth, live her truth—*be* her truth, and never let anyone ever take that from her, no matter what.

She studied her eyes carefully as she re-rimmed them with eyeliner and dabbed away her smudged mascara. Truth was, she had to admit the simple fact that she'd been so afraid of being alone, she'd allowed herself to completely compromise who she was. And in all truth, David had picked up on that fear, feeding off it like a predator and making her feel more and more like an imposter—which was the root of it all anyway.

From the time she'd been selected for the Better Chance program—which got her out of the New

York public school system for high school and into a top private boarding school in Connecticut, and ultimately propelled her into Vassar—she'd felt like an imposter, a person who didn't belong. She'd never fit into Choate with the rich kids who'd attended there without scholarships, just like she didn't really fit in socially at Vassar.

But no one and no programs helped smart kids from lean backgrounds fit in socially. That was up to each individual kid to wrestle with, and many lost the battle along the way. It wasn't the academics or their intellectual acumen that tanked their grades; it was the social pressure cooker that did it. She hadn't lost that battle academically; the inner fighter from el barrios made her dig in and tough it out with excellence. However, only just now did she realize that the struggle had left deep gashes in her self-esteem . . . and the one person who ever seemed to get that was a fellow veteran of cultural transplanting—Ryan.

When chosen for the honor to present with Dr. Cortland, she'd felt those same pangs of unworthiness. Since she was a little kid she'd always straddled two worlds: She felt good and cherished and smart within her family, but inept and so undeserving in the larger world beyond it.

"No more." Mia squared her shoulders, leaned forward, and spoke quietly and firmly to her reflection. "I *am* smart. I *know* what I'm talking about. I am *not* an imposter."

* * *

Ryan dropped his bags on the floor of his hotel room as Ethan and Ken got to their feet. They'd been lounging in the chairs in his room, waiting for him to arrive. All military formality was gone now among the three friends who had been through life and death and combat together. Only in front of the other members of the unit or before commanding officers did their friendship take on the formality of rank. But here, in the privacy of the hotel room, the three best friends were just guys who all went to West Point together.

Ethan reached him first with a strong handshake and a wide smile, then a ferocious bear hug. "Took you long enough."

Although the two almost stood eye-to-eye, Ethan was built like a baby rhino, a little shorter and squatter, his whole body corded with muscle that helped him lift Ryan up off his feet for a second.

"Glad to see your mangy ass, too," Ryan said, laughing, as they broke it up to turn to Ken. "And how'd you get into my room?"

Ken shrugged, looking down at Ryan from his six-foot-six vantage point. "All pro. You know that's what I do, man. By the way, who's the very cute female you were fraternizing with in the lobby?"

Ethan immediately whipped out his cell phone and pulled up Mia's photo. "Just downloaded from the lobby cameras, dude. She was with the four high-value assets, but man . . . her assets ain't bad, either."

"She's my in," Ryan said in a casual tone, trying not to bristle at his friends' description of Mia. He wheeled his heavy suitcase over to one of the beds and hoisted it up to begin unpacking artillery. "We have a little history. She's a research fellow of Cortland's and will be giving a portion of the presentation tomorrow. Expert in her field—"

"A little history?" Ken said, cutting him off with a smile. "Like . . . dude, there's history and then there's *his*-story. Which one, so we're clear?"

"Be serious," Ryan said, shaking his head as he continued to unpack. "I know her, all right—from the old days. She's good people. I want to ask her some questions after the lunch today, about the doctor's research, maybe find out if she knows who he's shared it with in greater detail than we might see at the conference. Basics."

"History," Ethan said, folding his bulky arms over his chest and cocking an eyebrow. "See, that's a word that's loaded like an HK416."

"Yeah. History," Ryan said in flat tone, keeping his focus on his suitcase. He'd known this line of questioning would come, and it was indeed logical, given the mission. That still didn't make him like it. But it was far better to have his guys aware of Mia than to ever compromise the mission by trying to keep them from knowing she existed. That would really muddy the waters.

"Does this historical female civilian know you're military?" Ken said, now leaning on the wall. His tone was still in the range of an amused buddy, but Ken's smile was fading. "That could pose a problem."

"It's a double-edged sword," Ryan admitted, looking up at Ken for a moment. "I've definitely considered that. The subject knows I used to be in the military—my cover was that I'm now affiliated with NYU. It's good that we have history so there's trust, but bad that she knew about that part of my career. However, I think I've dodged that bullet for now."

"There's that word *history* again that bothers me, bro," Ethan said shaking his head. "Like when you told her you were at NYU, no doubt as a friend, she'd introduce you around as her old friend from the old neighborhood, if she bumps into a colleague, right? And as you're aware, all those pocket-protector professors know one another. If you say you were newly hired, it's only a matter of time before they're gonna start playing the name game and when nobody knows who hired you . . ."

"Right," Ken said. "Definitely a problem, Captain."

Ryan looked from Ethan to Ken for a moment, now that Ken had used his formal rank in a statement. It was a verbal indicator that all the levity had bled out of the conversation. Now it was all about mission basics. Their eyes told him they respected his judgment but wondered if somehow it had gotten slightly skewed by this fine former friend. That troubled him, because in all truth, at this moment his conscience couldn't answer the charge.

"The subject was very into helping neighborhood kids, since she'd gotten a chance to get out of the old neighborhood by way of a solid minority program," Ryan said, looking at both his men. "So rather than claim I'm a new professor of geology or something crazy, where I could never pull off even a cursory conversation with the heavyweights at this conference, I could claim to be in a new outreach program that NYU has for minority youth—one that gets them interested in science. That's my story; that's why I'm here, to find out which professors at other universities might take some of our kids on . . . oh, hell, I don't know, maybe for semester exchanges or internships or something. Maybe to set up a graduate study pipeline for those who make it through NYU's undergrad programs, okay? It's an exploratory on NYU's dime, that's all she needs to know."

Ryan turned away from his men and sent his line of vision to the artillery in his suitcase. He could feel them exchange looks even as he gave them his back to stare at while he snapped an M4 out of the luggage housing.

"In any event, she trusts me due to history," Ryan pressed on when his buddies' silence wore on him. "I'll figure it out as I go along. Most likely there'll be no one here from any minority satellite program, and based on the VIP status of the professors here that thrive in the rarefied air of their respective institutions, those individuals are most likely not real familiar with the community outreach efforts of some lower-level, undergraduate department. That's not the focus of the universities in attendance. But I can always lean on the fact that I took rocks for jocks as a major, so it's very plausible that I'd be hired as a minority recruitment liaison to encourage inner-city kids to go into the sciences—and what better place to cruise for support and internships than at a conference where there's nothing but scientists?"

Ryan paused, hating that he'd become stiff and formal with his answer as though speaking to the brass. No doubt his buddies would sense the tension and the change and take that to the bank as a guarantee that the female subject was more than just an intel source.

"All right, Captain. Roger that," Ken said with a sheepish grin. "Adams and I will fall back, keep our eyes on the old men for the first twenty-four hours, and work in coordination with the feds and other branches of security here on the premises . . . while, you uh, gather intel—and if spotted, we will corroborate your cover. All of us are from humble beginnings and played ball, ran track, whatever—and we're now here as a part of a new program to focus on funneling minority youth into the sciences."

"Roger that," Ryan said crisply without looking up, not wanting to meet Ken's smiling eyes.

"But just as a clarification, I'm going back to this word *history*, Captain," Ethan said with a lopsided grin. "I know we have to plan on the fly, be flexible, and make it up as we go along . . . but this asset's dossier sounds really familiar to me."

Ken glanced at Ethan. "Like . . . she looks a lot different. But uhmmm . . . this wouldn't happen to be—"

"Yeah. It is, all right, but it doesn't make a difference. It wouldn't matter, and doesn't matter, who Cortland's research fellow is. That it happens to be Mia Austin is both coincidental and unfortunately circumstantial—but we're all here to do a job. We know he was one of the assets of value that were targeted, according to Patel, and we need to know if he's really got anything that the enemy can use. Period," Ryan said, turning away from his suitcase with annoyance.

After glaring at his friends for a moment, he ripped the zipper across the teeth of another hidden section in his luggage with one hard pull and then flung that section open to go into the hidden compartment.

"That's *Mia*?" Ethan's eyes got wide as he stared at Ken. "Holy Christ."

"Call in for backup," Ken said with a chuckle as he shook his head. "We've got a man down."

"Knock it off, assholes," Ryan grumbled. "That

was ten years ago. The main thing is, this woman can get us the vital intel we need without raising suspicions of the high-value assets or alerting any operatives here from al-Qaeda that we're on to their next potential move."

Ethan saluted Ryan with a smirk. "Roger that, Captain. Whatever you say."

CHAPTER 6

Ryan stepped off the crowded elevator and into the luncheon-bound throng. Although he kept his gaze scanning, his brain was also processing the truth. His men were right. Bumping into Mia could have created a catastrophic chain of events. Something as simple as his name badge could have caused her to publicly question him, had he chosen to register under a fictitious name, for instance. But because he always opted for the simplest course of action, RYAN MASON was emblazoned on the plastic-covered badge now firmly pinned to his jacket lapel.

The moment he entered the room he spotted her leisurely talking to the four professors he and his unit had their eyes on. She was way up front in the VIP section of reserved tables. Cool. A brief nod and a moment of eye contact was all he had to share once she spotted him. For now that was also all his nervous system could probably handle.

Drs. Walter Cooper and Anatoly Ivanov had made
it. Ryan's line of vision swept the room and locked
with Ken's and then Ethan's. Ken replied with a
subtle nod, letting him know he'd also seen the two
additional professors on their assets-of-value list.
All six were here. Hotel records would be pulled
by the feds to see whom they'd checked in with so
anyone close to them would be protected. Ryan
watched Ethan discreetly move toward a federal
agent off to the stage left of the ballroom. The suit
nodded and then walked away. Everything was a
matter of quiet choreography.

Between FBI and the coordinated efforts with
Homeland Security and intelligence, those professors and their families would be safeguarded, while
the tip of the spear within his unit followed the lead
to the sleeper cell lying low on the East Coast.

Filing through the guest admittance line, Ryan
found a table of nobody-special guests and lingered. Not one face in the crowd was on the watch
list. There had to be easily three hundred to five
hundred people in the ballroom. Nada. Even the
staff, whom he scrutinized thoroughly, didn't fit
the bill. But his gut told him that something prob-
lematic was near.

Still uneasy as the guests were asked to take
their seats, Ryan watched water glasses being filled
at the large round tables that each held ten guests.
It was so easy to abduct someone. A dry coffee cup
in a hotel room could be laced with a tasteless,

clear substance that would activate the moment liquid hit it. Chloroforming an elderly man in a vacant hotel men's room, then quickly hoisting him to an exit . . . there were a million ways to get the job done. It didn't have to be a loud, violent body grab. Most sophisticated operators who wanted the person alive for a ransom or a strategic purpose wouldn't do that.

They'd all been over the backgrounds and bios of the entire hotel desk staff and cleaning staff three times to ensure that no one they didn't know would have access to the professors' rooms. Sweeper teams were on patrol to monitor the hallways on the corridors where each key professor's room was located. But what was he missing? Why were his nerves so wire-tight?

Ryan scanned the room again. This time his gaze lingered on Mia for a moment, and she looked up. She gave him a small wave and a shrug. Reading the silent message transmitted in her lovely eyes, he knew what she was saying without needing to hear the words: *Why didn't you come find me, I would have made room at our table for you.* He lifted one shoulder with a half smile, letting her know it was more than okay. She nodded and then waved good-bye as the speaker quieted the room.

Wow . . . she'd gotten it. They'd had an entire conversation across a ballroom filled with five hundred noisy people without the aid of text messaging or words. Ryan picked at the salad he didn't want, wondering if he'd ever find that level of pure simplicity with another woman . . . that mesh of understanding; the ability to communicate everything and nothing all with one look. After a decade of searching, he already knew the answer.

Mia picked at her salad, trying to keep her stomach from doing flip-flops. Yes, it was definitely best for Ryan to be seated very far away from her or she would have been a pure ball of nerves at the table. Small talk was normally easy in the company of the professors, but at the moment she was having too much trouble concentrating on their esoteric topics of debate. She was just glad the speakers had begun. That gave her a reason to remain quiet without seeming rude.

But sitting through the droning monotony of sponsors and accolades being giving out by pre-conference speakers was going to make her climb out of her skin.

From a sidelong glance she allowed her gaze to travel toward Ryan's table, but then sat up a bit, flustered when she saw David come in late and slide in to sit at an adjacent open table.

This could *not* be happening.

Not that Ryan would ever know. Not that David would say a word to the man. This was her own private meltdown moment. She'd known that David would probably be here. In fact she'd braced herself for it months ago. But now that he was here and now that it was all so very real, a hundred thoughts crowded into her mind at once.

Half of her wanted feminine revenge, wanted to let David know just how much he'd hurt her over the years and how now she was doing so much better without him. Then the more rational part of her just wanted him to go away.

After a few shaky moments, the realist in her took over and won the internal battle. David Williams would never be caught dead saying anything to her in public around their mutual professional colleagues that could be misconstrued as a snipe. He was too much into the politics of achievement, and since she was a so-called rising star, he'd most likely save any character assassination for his guarded personal circles. And Ryan had *nothing whatsoever* to do with any of that.

But before she could jerk her attention away from David, he'd caught her gaze and then inclined his head with a knowing, sarcastic smirk. It was all she could do not to roll her eyes at the man. Mia went back to her salad refusing to even acknowledge his presence. The sonofabitch had called her every low-life name in the book when she'd handed him back his ring, and had been so virulent that at one point she feared he might strike her again. That had been enough to make her flee and refuse his calls, mark his letters RETURN TO SENDER, and basically cut off all communication. Her reasoning was basic: If he'd gone there before she was his wife, then the dude had anger management issues that she wasn't about to stick around to see.

The one thing she hadn't acknowledged within herself, however, was the tight and horrible feeling she'd have in the pit of her stomach when she finally did see him. Yes, it was safe in this very public forum, and yes it was doubtful that he'd make a fool of himself by getting loud or untoward while at a professional conference. But it meant that the period of silence she'd enjoyed once he finally stopped his harassment campaign could be over. Suddenly she didn't want broiled salmon or baked chicken. Really she wanted fresh air, but there was no way to escape the ballroom without having to pass him. For now, she'd have to endure by staying put and listening to whomever was droning away at the lectern.

Mia faced forward, giving David her back, and tried not to allow her mind to spiral into ever-darkening thoughts.

He knew something was wrong. Very wrong. His gut never lied to him.

Ryan watched Mia's easy body language stiffen. Her complexion almost seemed to drain its once glorious caramel-bronze color to appear near ashen for a second. Her gaze had hardened in a way he'd never seen in it before, and he followed her line of vision to the point of her apparent disturbance, and then stopped. Hmmm. Business or professional disdain, or both?

Visually assessing the man who'd clearly unnerved Mia, Ryan embedded him into his mental database of faces to watch. Tall, approximately six foot two. Midforties. Short, wavy hair—salt and pepper. Clean-shaven. Not wearing glasses, but probably had in contacts or had potentially undergone laser surgery. Designer suit. Hugo Boss. Cole Haan shoes. Came in late, but welcomed at the table—made an entrance of importance. Personality assessment: vain amid his colleagues.

Although he'd kept his attention sweeping the room, only half listening to the speakers, he watched Mia. Her smile had returned but now seemed forced. She only pushed around the salmon on her plate, taking just a few bites. She seemed to focus a little too hard on the very boring speakers. And as the luncheon broke up, she lingered a little too long at her table. Yeah, his gut never lied to him.

Moving through the crowd, he abandoned his original plan to text her and wait for her in the lobby. Their eyes met as she looked up, and her easy smile returned. But he also noticed that her shoulders dropped about an inch in what appeared to be relief. Huh? Okay. The closer he got to her, the wider her smile became. Then she unexpectedly reached forward and grabbed his arm once he was close enough.

"Dr. Cortland," she said, almost breathing out the words, "this is a very dear friend of mine, Ryan Mason, who is now at NYU in their Geology Department."

"Well, then," Dr. Cortland said with a welcoming smile, "if you've been vetted by Mia, Dr. Mason, then it is my pleasure to meet you—and perhaps you can be an impartial referee on an argument we've been having about the seismic activity in Yellowstone National Park of late?"

Ryan laughed and held up both hands before his chest. "No, no, a few points of clarification. I'm not a PhD or in the Geology Department. I'm with a program that helps steer minority youth into the sciences, and—"

"That's *fabulous*," Mia said, gushing. "Ryan, that so suits you."

"Indeed it is a very worthy and honorable cause," Dr. Cortland said, nodding in agreement. He turned to his colleagues with a wise smile. "Then I guess we old men will have to find another arbiter."

"Yes," Dr. Albright said, shaking Ryan's hand. "But after we escape and nap for a few hours."

They all laughed as Ryan made the introductory rounds. Following the retinue of elderly professors out of the ballroom, he noticed that the man in the back seemed to be lingering by the exit doors, and Mia's unease had immediately returned.

"How about that walk?" Ryan asked quietly, leaning down to place the private suggestion in

Mia's ear. "You look like you could use some fresh air after this luncheon."

She stopped, turned, and gazed up at him. "I really could," she said and then hesitated, glancing at the door. "But can I change out of this monkey suit into some sneakers and jeans . . . I'm just . . ."

"Sure," he said, giving the guy at the door a sidelong glance and not at all liking how he was staring at him. "I'll wait for you in the lobby."

"Okay," she said in a soft tone, but he noticed she hadn't moved.

"The dude by the door—is he a problem?"

"Oh, no, Ryan, I'm sorry. That's—"

"It's cool, Mia. Listen, how about if I walk you to the elevators, ride up on your floor, and hang out in the little area on your floor, where there's a sofa by the elevators? Then . . . I'll go to my room—you hang in the hall just outside my door, and talk to me through the door so I know you're safe, all right?" He winked at her as her gorgeous mouth tried to suppress a smile.

"It's not all that bad, Ryan. I'm not in jeopardy or anything . . . just a little uncomfortable and being silly. I apologize."

"Tell me about it, or not, while we walk. I've got water under my bridge, too," he said, not taking no for an answer. "But riding up to your floor so that some jerk doesn't make you feel uncomfortable and so you can avoid a confrontation is no big deal. I'm okay with that and I already know you may take half an hour to put on some jeans. But you know that it'll take me . . . what . . . thirty seconds to rip off a suit and throw on some jeans and a T-shirt, right?"

"Yeah," she said, now laughing.

"That's because you're a girl and I'm—"

"Superman," she said, offering him a sexy wink.

Embarrassed but pleased by her flirtatious comment, he used a chuckle as a cover. "If you say so."

She winked at him, totally catching him off guard. "I know so."

He had no response. He hadn't expected that at all, not after ten years. Wow . . . okay . . . just be cool, man.

But something instinctive and protective and territorial made him place a flat palm at her back and use his body as a shield between her and the guy at the door as they passed him. He felt Mia stiffen as her chin lifted and she walked a little bit faster. He could feel her breath quicken, as though she was slightly terrified. Yeah, this was personal. Very personal, which meant it could get ugly.

Ryan gave the man by the exit a *back off or die* look. Not even Delta Force training could have stopped the primal directive: female in distress from an encroaching male. The bastard had a target on his forehead if he'd said one thing out of order to the lady as she'd passed.

The moment they reached the elevators, her entire body relaxed. She looked up at him with the biggest, brownest, most trusting eyes, her voice suddenly lowering with her long lashes to a delicate whisper, and said three words that completely compromised him.

"Thank you, Ryan."

CHAPTER 7

The crush of the crowded elevator ensured that Mia's body stayed within dangerous proximity of his. He could detect a light, fresh fragrance wafting off her hair. Military discipline was probably the only thing that kept him from lowering his nose to it and inhaling deeply with his eyes closed. Instead he stood at attention, kept his eyes on the ascending numbers, and firmly jammed his hands in his pockets.

He didn't need to allow his palm to settle into that familiar, gentle sway in her back again. Didn't need the tactile stimulation of the fabric that covered what he knew to be the unparalleled softness of her skin.

"You sure you want to do this?" she asked with a shy smile as the doors opened.

The question snapped his focus back to the crowded elevator car as a few men lowered their gazes with a smile.

"No problem," he replied, trying to force all-business into his tone while ignoring the obviously incorrect assumptions being made by the other passengers. He could've sworn he'd heard someone mutter, "Lucky bastard," as the doors closed, and was just glad that Mia hadn't.

Finally out of the claustrophobic enclosure, he followed Mia to her room. Nervous energy made the muscles in his stomach contract as though waiting on a gut punch that never came.

"I promise to make it a quick change," she said, stopping in front of her door and producing a card key. "I really appreciate all of this and you really didn't have to do it. I was just being—"

"No apologies. Go put on your jeans and I'll be down the hall," he said, not allowing her to deride herself.

"Right," she murmured. "I remember. No apologies." Then she slipped into her room and shut the door between them.

He stood there for a few moments, slowly realizing how the Freudian comment had so easily rolled off his tongue. *No apologies* had been their motto . . . no apologies for wanting each other as passionately as they had; no apologies for making each other first in their lives when friends and family couldn't find them for two weeks. No apologies for choosing the call of their careers when it was over.

Ryan made a crisp, military about-face turn on

his heel and headed back down the hall. What the hell was he doing?

When he reached the elevator bay, sitting on the small padded bench was nearly impossible, but he forced himself not to pace. Each time a room door opened and slammed he steeled himself and refused to look around the corner like an eager teenager, yet was always disappointed that it was only the hotel's housekeeping staff simply going about their daily routine.

To his surprise, Mia emerged from her room after only ten minutes—ten interminable minutes when he'd had to remember to breathe. But when she appeared around the alcove corner to join him at the elevators, for a moment his voice caught in his throat.

The transformation was heart-stopping. In ten minutes she'd let down her silky profusion of auburn hair, making his fingers ache to allow it to flow between them. She'd ditched her glasses and her mouth now glistened a kissable peach. Small gold hoops made him want to toy with her earlobes as he took her mouth. Gone was the suit; she now had on a pretty peach tank top that showed off the real curves her business attire hid. In that moment he decided, she always needed to wear jeans around him—good God Almighty. How could a woman become a totally different person in just ten little minutes? Had he known such an awesome feat was possible, he would have gladly waited an hour.

"Sorry it took me so long," she said, coming up to him with a big smile.

He wanted to say *Wow,* but opted for a casual comeback. "Ten minutes, not bad. You're giving women a good name. I'm impressed."

She laughed and gave his arm a playful shove. All he could do was laugh to keep from crying as he pressed the elevator button. She was wearing Angel, his favorite scent on her. That was the sucker punch he'd been waiting for, and it practically knocked the wind out of him with the sudden rush of memory.

Then it dawned on him—she definitely didn't need to know where his room was. Stupid, stupid, stupid! No telling what was actually going to go down in the hotel.

Remaining in character, he frowned and then said, "Hold up. What am I doing?"

She looked at him with a question in her eyes.

"Man . . . you don't keep a fine woman standing outside your room waiting in the danged hall. Okay, on this I owe you an apology. My bad."

Now she laughed hard. He'd slipped into old neighborhood slang to put her at ease and to strengthen their memory bond. What might seem like a lame excuse to her actually had true merit; it was just impossible to explain that right now.

"Ryan . . . this is the twenty-first century," she argued, shaking her head. "I can wait the all of five minutes it would probably take you to change."

"No. Not having it. For real. I should have had a better plan than you cooling your heels in a dag-gone hallway. Can you tell I'm a little rusty and was making it up as I went along when I saw you getting tight around that dude by the door?" Ryan theatrically shook his head. "Come with me," he went on, giving her his arm and leading her away from the elevators toward her room. He stopped in front of her door. "True chivalry demands that you hang out for five minutes in your room while I go change. Then I'll come back here for you."

"But—"

"No buts," he said, lifting and turning his head in mock offense. Although her laughter was infec-tious, he tried to keep a straight face as mirth made her eyes sparkle with mischief. He waited until she finally complied with his request and dug in her jeans pocket for her room key. But he continued his self-directed rant to keep her laughing.

"What are you nuts, Mason?" he muttered loud enough for her to hear, causing her to laugh even harder as she opened the door. "I am really, really out of touch . . . dang. Just pitiful."

Her mirth followed him down the hall as he rounded the corner and called the elevator again. Oh, yeah, he'd dodged a bullet—good thing Mia was a good sport. This was insane. Correction: *I'm insane*.

Pacing now, he needed something to do to spend the excess energy. The stairs were an option, but the last thing he needed was to go through a fire exit that locked on reentry or to run into one of his men or something.

But elevators at a hotel that was hosting a large conference were always a bottleneck to movement. So he had to wait. It annoyed him that it would probably take longer to get down to his room and back than it would to change. Regardless, the hotel wasn't big enough for him and Mia to be sharing while he was working. In fact, all of freakin' New York City wasn't big enough.

Thankfully, before his nerves frayed and snapped the elevator came—and he almost said a Hail Mary that Ken and Ethan were nowhere in the vicinity to witness his temporary insanity.

Ryan jogged down the corridor the moment the elevator doors opened and entered his room as though someone was chasing him. In a flash he ripped off his suit and threw on a pair of jeans and collared golf shirt, then spent all of ten seconds deciding between penny loafers and running shoes. Running shoes won out. The entire process took under three minutes, which was a good thing considering that, had he spent time truly thinking about it, he might have done the logical thing and bailed. But his mind wasn't in a logical mood and he'd developed enough convoluted justifications for continuing with what he called a fact-finding mission that he was on autopilot by now.

* * *

Mia walked back and forth within her room and then sat down on the bed, only to pop up quickly and check her lip gloss in the mirror for the third time. With her nervous system on overload, every time she heard someone walk down the hall she forgot to breathe. The hotel cleaning staff schedule was wreaking havoc with her mind. After a moment she caught herself straining to listen for the light elevator chime that was impossible to hear from her room.

"Just stop," she whispered to herself and closed her eyes, and then sat down very slowly in the chair adjacent to the bed.

Ryan would be here soon, they'd walk around a bit, catch up on old times, have a beer, and then she had to get back to her room—solo—to prepare for the big debut presentation she had in the morning. Simple. Besides, time changed people. Time changed circumstances. If she were honest, she really didn't know this man and he really didn't know her. At least, that was what she told herself to keep her runaway emotions in check.

But a light knock on the door practically made her jump out of her skin. Up in a flash, she then forced herself to slow down and singsonged the words, "Just a minute."

All she could do was smile at Ryan, who stood before her checking his watch as though he was an Olympic time judge.

"How'd I do?"

"I can't believe you're already changed and back," she said, laughing. "Didn't you just get on the elevator?"

"That was the bottleneck. Could've improved on my timing, but there was this convention, yada, yada, yada . . ."

She shook her head and entered the hallway with him feeling that old camaraderie, that comfort of being with someone familiar enter her pores and soak into her bones. As much as the man turned her on, there was also something real, and warm, and mellow, and good about him. Around Ryan she didn't have to guard every word or worry about being socially or politically correct. As they walked down the hall in companionable silence, she also realized that, for Ryan, she didn't have to be perfect. Just the way she was had always been good enough for him.

That sudden, quiet realization briefly put tears in her eyes, but she blinked them away before he could see them. If he had, she would have claimed allergies. Anyway, how did you explain to someone you hadn't seen in ten years how the simple act of acceptance felt so very right and good?

Okay, Mia, she said to herself, *keep it light.*

"So what sessions are you going to?" Ryan asked, pressing the button and stepping back to look at her.

Glad for the reprieve from her own thoughts, Mia released a long sigh. "After I get through my presentation tomorrow, I'll probably follow the tracks on seismic activity. But to be honest, I've been so nervous about getting ready for that talk that I really haven't focused on which will be the best ones to go to. You?"

"Wait a minute," he said, measuring his words. "*You're* giving a talk tomorrow?"

Before she could get defensive, his face lit up with a huge smile.

"Oh, my God, Mia . . . that is just awesome. You must be totally proud."

"Totally freaked out is a more accurate description, but thank you."

The elevator came and saved her further comment.

"You have to give me the full rundown on how this all happened while we walk," he said, ushering her into the nearly full elevator ahead of him.

"Not much to tell, save a lot of boring interdepartmental politics—I'll spare you the details," she replied over her shoulder.

"I want a full after-action report," he said and then fell quiet as the doors closed behind them.

Ryan looked at the numbers. *An after-action report?* Was he *nuts* using military speak in public, with her, in a crowded elevator?

Oh, this was beyond sloppy; it had now crossed over into the realm of being dangerous. After this walk and a little intel gathering, he needed to disengage. He could always promise to explain everything to her later, but he had to regain his focus.

The elevator sounded for the lobby floor and once the doors opened, everyone piled out as though living sardines escaping a tight tin can. Ryan motioned with his chin toward the opposite direction from the throng's flow.

"Let's head out the back door and go up Washington to Liberty, then roll on over to Trinity Place and get on the other side of this crowd."

"Sounds like you've already scoped this place out," she said, following him as he ushered her through the lobby.

"Yeah, something like that."

But as they walked by packed hotel restaurants and stands of people gathered in small clusters to catch up and gab, he felt her tense as they passed the Starbucks near the back hotel exit. With one hand on the glass door, he swung it open for her, but his gaze quickly perused the long coffee line. The guy that made her nervous was there, standing with his back to the exit. However, he'd obviously caught Mia's reflection in the window. His attention was focused on her from a sidelong glance; the muscle in his jaw was pulsing. The scowl on his face made Ryan linger just long enough to catch the guy's eye. Male-to-male eye contact communicated everything: *Step to her and your ass is mine.* Then Ryan stepped through the door.

He almost had to jog to catch up with Mia, and

didn't comment on her brisk pace as they'd walked beneath extensive scaffolding and reached the bright blue World Trade Center construction site boarding. He knew she had to walk it off, whatever bad feelings the jerk at the conference kindled within her.

Just keeping pace with her strides, but making sure that he didn't crowd her, he said nothing as they cleared the Ground Zero area, heading away from the American Stock Exchange and Trinity Church, up to Church, Dey, and Fulton Streets past the Century 21 department store, and then passed the Federal Building heading east on Barclay toward West Broadway.

He really hadn't planned a route, but this one was as good as any. When they had to stop to wait for traffic, he used that as an opportunity to get Mia to slow down.

"So, you doing the Boston or the New York," he said, trying to sound serious but allowing a half smile.

"The Boston or New York? I don't follow?"

"The marathon. Figured you must be in training."

She stopped for a moment, even though they now had the light, and then shook her head with a sad smile. "Hey . . . I'm sorry."

"No apologies. Remember?"

"Yeah, I do," she said in a much calmer voice, and she took a more leisurely pace as they crossed the street. "You must really think I'm crazy by now."

"Nope," he said, walking alongside her and then crossing around her to get her on the inside of the curb. "I just think there's some really messed-up history with that guy who keeps giving you the evil eye . . . and I think that he's gonna make some of my old bad habits from Bed-Stuy come out if he doesn't stop giving you the grisly. Wasn't that long ago that I could have wound up in juvenile detention if I didn't have a praying momma."

She laughed, and he was so glad that she did.

"He's just a social irritant, not dangerous," she said, slowing her pace enough so that they could now walk and talk. "He's pissed off that I'm doing a presentation that he thinks he should have been chosen to do."

"Then . . . ah . . . it's just professional hateration," Ryan said with a sly smile.

"That and," she replied, with a wide grin without looking at him.

"Okaaay. Cool. So, he got passed over for the spotlight. Shit happens. He needs to get over it. Besides, this much I know about you, Mia—you got the opportunity on merit. Nobody I know works harder than you do."

She tilted her head to consider him, looking at him with a shy but pleased expression.

"Thank you, Ryan. You saying that means a lot to me."

"Just telling the truth as I see it."

"Well, some people don't think very much of my

research or professional skills," she said, releasing a long sigh. "Fact is, I'd been working with my mentor, Dr. Cortland, a long time on my theory that naturally occurring phenomena could be weaponized, especially earthquakes in major cities. *Some people* laughed at me and thought the idea was a quack one, but not Dr. Cortland. At one point I was accused of watching too many sci-fi movies or reading too many comics. But once Dr. Cortland got behind my theory and validated it as a possibility, and his colleagues began to also look into the potential, things started to get strained between David and me."

"Professionally," Ryan said, asking the question without asking the question.

But apparently Mia decoded the one-word statement, because her next answer broadened her pretty smile.

"Both."

"Well, like I said—he needs to get over it." Ryan paused, needing to drill down into her research but not wanting to make her feel like she was being mentally stalked. "So, in truth, this was really your theory . . . and these other scientists launched research into the area after you?"

"I know, I know," she said, waving her hands. "Seems incredible, and most people don't know that. They think the more distinguished gentlemen are the experts in this brand-new potential threat to humankind, but they're not."

She stopped and laughed hard, and he simply stared at her, both fearful now for her safety and thoroughly intrigued. "See, most people have been led to believe that conspiracy theory kooks—you know, the stereotypical guys out in the Rocky Mountains somewhere who live off the grid and have a portable CB radio—are the nut jobs coming up with this stuff. No serious scientist has staked his or her career on the outlander types of research lately. So when small circles within the established scientific community started talking about it, the theory got quickly assigned to Dr. Cortland and his colleagues . . . not the research fellow whom everyone thinks just goes to fetch coffee or whatever."

"That's so wild," Ryan said, staring at her with a sobered expression. "So . . . like the other doctors, the ones you're working for, they're feeding off your research—not the other way around."

"You could put it that way," she said and then began walking with a broad smile lighting up her face. "I'm not trying to toot my own horn, believe me. But it's just little ol' me that's poured a lot of time and energy into this very speculative area of research right now. No other serious scientists, especially ones with outstanding careers, would initially touch it. They were focused on climate change, the natural phenomena of the earth's changes, and how we're polluting the planet. But no one was looking at how to weaponize natural phenomena, except weather—

which is outside of my bailiwick and there are entire cadres of scientists dealing with it . . . but it got me thinking—if they could weaponize the weather or were trying to anyway, then why not other stuff, you know?"

Ryan just nodded for a moment, almost unable to absorb what he was hearing while also processing the incalculable danger she was in. "So Dr. Cortland allowed you to go down this path on your own?"

"Yep," she said in an excited tone, clearly pleased that she could open up and talk to him about her work. "Once I made the argument to Dr. Cortland, he was intrigued and allowed me the professional freedom to really delve into what could happen if a loose nuke or even a conventional warhead were to be placed near known fault lines and tectonic plates. So, under his name, I began working long-distance with Dr. Patel in Pakistan, Dr. Albright in London, Dr. Molefi in Ghana, Dr. Lee in China, and Dr. Ivanov in Russia—leading scientists in the area of seismology. The Internet is a beautiful thing, and I was so thrilled to be given access to Dr. Cortland's inner circle."

By now Mia was so into the story that she was gesturing with her graceful hands as they walked and she talked.

"In fact, Dr. Patel was the first one who really signed on to support me, and he immediately got the implications . . . maybe because of the tensions in his region. He helped me the most and I so hope he gets here so we can finally meet face-to-face. Up till now we've been doing Cisco teleconferences. But David was livid with jealousy. *The* Dr. Williams felt that I was not only diverting institutional funds for a frivolous project, but also somehow professionally embarrassing him because of our other affiliation."

"So, this is your theory . . . ," Ryan said carefully. "Completely. Down to the last detail?"

"Uh-huh," she said in a cheerful tone, striding beside him with confidence.

Jesus H. Christ . . . this is who Patel was getting his key information from? Why hadn't he mentioned Mia and only the other older scientists? Was it some kind of professional oversight, or was it ego that led Patel to believe the data had to be coming from Cortland and not a young female? Was it some kind of cultural thing, where brilliant females couldn't guide a male in his field, especially an older male?

"Like . . . I'm trying to wrap my mind around this, Mia. This is all you, and these old dudes were supporting you in *your* research?"

Ryan's mind was racing as he waited for Mia's answer. But he noticed an immediate change in her expression, and then mentally doubled back on his question. Maybe he'd pressed too hard.

"Yeah. I know it's hard to believe . . ." She stopped

again and frowned this time, suddenly seeming as though she didn't trust him.

"It's not hard to believe," he replied quickly, not wanting her to think he doubted her talent. But her expression went from defensive to sad.

"You're not going to get weird on me now, are you?"

Compelled by her sad tone, he reached out without thinking and touched her cheek. "No, I'm not going to get weird on you because you're brilliant, Mia. I'm just blown away, is all."

She stared up at him, her shy smile returning with something he dared not name.

"Good," she murmured, and then broke his trance when his hand fell away by starting to walk and slowly talk again. "It's been my experience that guys get weird sometimes when they know a girl has been to see the wizard to get a brain."

"Over the years I've been blamed for a lot of things by women, but not that," he said laughing.

She nodded, her smile never diminishing. "I downplayed my role in developing the hypothesis, initially, because it was causing so much havoc for me personally—and I didn't want to step on any toes professionally. But then when I gave a presentation on how a tsunami could be created in the Azores to lash the East Coast and all of Dr. Cortland's colleagues concurred that it was extremely plausible, Dr. Cortland said I must present that information along with my Manhattan theory at this world conference. Haiti had just happened and Chile, plus the president had just had his Nuclear Summit to try to put a guardrail around loose nukes, and suddenly what was going to be my little late-afternoon talk suddenly got bumped to a prime spot in the conference. Timing probably had as much to do with it all as did the actual research."

Mia let out a deep sigh. "But even before my talk got moved to the top of the key, David was so out-raged that he'd been working at the Smithsonian years before me without the kind of recognition I was getting that he left in a professional snit and took a position at Columbia University—much to his family's chagrin. He hated the move, they hated the move, and of course it was all my fault that he had to move in the first place. They're all from DC. Old, established, DC. Need I say more?"

Ryan just shook his head, pure adrenaline now spiking through his system. "No. Not at all, Mia. I get it."

CHAPTER 8

Mia fell quiet, suddenly feeling self-conscious. She hadn't meant to rattle on about office politics or the pathetic state of her love life. It was just that Ryan was so easy to talk to, and from the expression of genuine worry that haunted his handsome face, he truly seemed to care.

But Camille and her older sister had warned her about being such a geek and taking over light dating conversation with her brain—which was exactly why, according to her love advisers as well as all the magazines she'd read on the subject, men shied away from her once she opened her mouth. It was time to shift gears before she totally blew the groove, as Camille would say.

"Enough about me, what about you?" Mia forced a light casual tone into her voice as they pressed toward Warren Street.

"Not much to tell," Ryan replied with an easy

shrug. "Did my stint in the military. Traveled the world. I went. I saw. Then I came home."

She had to laugh. "You went, you saw, you conquered, and you came home. That sums up ten years?"

"Pretty much," he said, now laughing. "You know me, Mia. I'm a man of few words. Suffice to say that it's not a glamorous job. Lots of real hellhole places to be stationed at don't warrant discussion."

"But what about when you got leave?" she said, sweeping her arms wide with dramatic flair that really made his spectacular smile widen.

"Okay . . . China was breathtaking. Huge and clean and so old that it defies description. It's one of those you've-gotta-see-it-for-yourself kinds of places on the planet, like the temples of Cambodia. They have these trees that have grown up and over and around the temples, so big that the temple is actually built into the tree. And Egypt . . . man . . . seeing the size of what people built without technology. It'll make you believe in aliens, will make you feel so tiny and insignificant standing beside the toes of a statue."

"Wow . . . ," she murmured. "I've only been an armchair traveler, really. I've been to a few national geological hot spots and that one big trip overseas," she said, suddenly sorry she'd mentioned Indonesia, the last thing that had come between them. "But," she said, recovering smoothly, "I'm glad you got to go to a lot of the places you've always dreamed of."

Ryan ran a palm over his short-cropped hair. "Yeah, I spent my leaves trying to do my bucket list of places to go and places to see, I guess because in my line of work I never knew when it was gonna be my last day alive. So you tend to do stuff other people put off for later."

They fell silent for the rest of the block. It didn't need to be said that she wished she could have been there with him on those trips. He also seemed to be temporarily consumed with his own thoughts. She just wondered what really lucky woman had been able to be a part of his world tour.

As they approached the corner and then waited for the traffic to pass, he turned to her. "You know, I'd love to go to all those places again so I could really appreciate them. Something was missing the first time around."

"Like what?" she asked, now curious.

"You," he said in a very mellow tone, and then gently escorted her across the street.

"There's a Whole Foods," he said, not allowing her mind to recover.

"Oh, yeah, cool," she said, still reeling from his previous comment.

"Wanna go in and get some stuff for the hotel?"

She didn't know what to say for a second.

"You know—munchies that are really good,

versus the crap they sell for an outrageous price in the gift shop."

"Yeah, cool," she said, trying to hide the fact that her heart was beating a path out of her chest.

This was déjà vu. After the first night of hard lovemaking, and paying a small fortune in room service for mediocre food, they'd escaped to locate a supermarket and gone shopping for fruit, snacks, and juice, and bottled waters . . . and they'd laughed in the aisles, and kissed, and gotten hotter for each other as he stocked up with the promise to hold her hostage within the confines of the room until their rations ran out. And he'd made good on that promise, leaving her limp, ragged, and happy. She wondered if he remembered, or if it was just her feminine wishful thinking.

A blast of cool supermarket air hit him—and good thing, too. He needed that in the worst way.

Commandeering a cart, he waved his free hand out toward the endless aisles that lay before them. "Lady's choice. I'll be your pack mule."

"Well, what do you want?"

He paused. There were two ways to answer that question, but only one was appropriate. "How about fruit to start, then we segue from there to decadent?"

She laughed. "From fruit to cookies."

"Precisely. Then we've gotta throw in some chips. Can't have sweet without the salty."

"Maaan . . . don't even go there."

Now he laughed and headed toward the produce. How did this woman make a mundane chore like going to the supermarket a turn-on? His memory was really leaning into a dangerous area now, when it should have remained firmly in the green zone. But just watching her sashay up to the oranges, pick one up, squeeze it, then smell it made his mouth go dry. Oh, yeah, he remembered that her favorite way to eat fruit was naked, in bed, and as a way to get quick sugar back into her bloodstream after being thoroughly spent.

"How many do you want?"

"Huh?" It took him a second to process her question. "Oh, uhmmm . . . I don't know . . . maybe like three or four?"

She smiled what seemed like a knowing smile and turned back to the stand. But maybe that was his interpretation getting in the way. Maybe it was just a normal smile. Oh, shit, he was really messed up right now and couldn't tell. *Fall back, soldier,* he told himself and left her to go find a few apples. He needed a little space to recover. But she came up behind him and he felt the heat from her body shadowing his before she even touched his shoulder.

"Want to taste something sweet?" she said, offering him a bit of honeydew melon on the end of a toothpick.

She'd obviously found a samples table nearby, but for some reason he couldn't take his eyes off her mouth and the way it moved as she chewed the bit of melon she'd popped in. Hell yeah, he wanted to taste something sweet.

"Is it good?" he asked, his voice bottoming into a murmur as she held the fruit out to him.

Her smile had begun to fade as she nodded. "Yes," she said just above a whisper.

He leaned down and forced his mouth to take the piece of melon instead of her mouth, but covered her hand with his to guide it to his lips. After pulling the meaty cube off the toothpick, he let her hand go and nodded.

"You were right."

She backed up a little and then looked away shyly. "It's just a shame there's nowhere to store one of these once it's cut, but I couldn't pass it up."

"I hear you," he murmured, his hand still burning from where it had connected to her skin. "Then maybe we should move to decadent and get you some chocolate chip cookies."

"Oh, see . . . I can't believe you even went there," she said, spinning around and backing down the aisle. "I need those like I need a hole in my head."

"What are you talking about?" he said, catching up to her merry stride.

"I've given up on three-thousand-calorie cookies that'll keep me in the gym for a week. I have a desk job now, and it all goes south."

He couldn't help the comment or the smirk that

went with it. "Let's get you a baker's dozen then . . . because from where I stand, it's all good."

All right, he had to kick his old Bed-Stuy ways to the curb and stop thinking about the one thing that wasn't going to happen. But she laughed. The woman laughed. She didn't look upset, offended, or like she was ready to bolt. That was beyond dangerous.

"Okay, maybe *one*," she said, leading him toward the bakery section.

That was all he wanted was one . . . one good go-hard one more time for old times' sake, didn't she understand that? Then again, even that was a lie. He wanted more than one. More like that baker's dozen, for as many years. But there was no way to explain that as she stood in front of the homemade cookies with her arms folded, trying to scowl.

"See, you're trying to tempt me, and I'm trying to be good."

He so badly wanted to ask her if she was talking about cookies or something else.

"I need a partner in crime, since my willpower is shot." It was true, but she didn't need to know that his mind was tracking way past baked goods.

"Nope," she said, laughing.

"Aw, girl, you mean to tell me you don't have my back?"

She laughed harder and danced away from the cookies, and then lingered for a moment with her forefinger pressed to her lips.

"Okay. I see how you do me," he said, taking her back to the old days with the easy style of neighborhood teasing. "You're gonna make me go hardcore and find the chips—kettle chips."

"Noooo," she said, laughing hard as she placed her hands on her hips and tossed her head back. "Don't you dare!"

"Oh, yeah I am," he said, running with the cart down the aisle. "Might get ice cream, too, since nobody has my back."

"It'll melt," she called out behind him, giggling as she chased him.

"And what? So."

"Get out of the chips aisle."

"Look . . . they've got barbecue, sea salt and cracked pepper—"

"Just stop," she said, turning away and putting her fingers in her ears. "La la la la la—I can't hear you."

His phone vibrated in his pocket as he rounded the aisle. Looking three ways to be sure that Mia wouldn't see him, he took the encrypted text: *Chatter on lines has her name embedded. Look alive.*

Instantly sobered, he turned down the next aisle to catch up with Mia. Then he forced himself to laugh. She knew him too well, and he'd have to really work hard to keep his worry concealed. Her name had come up on terrorist radar. Until he knew how, he wasn't going to leave her side. She could have been mentioned as a conference addition, an assistant or intern to the older professors who were known targets—or she could now be a target. Not knowing was kicking his ass.

Ryan came out of a nearby aisle, belly-laughing at her antics. He rounded her with a bag of sour-cream-and-onion-flavored chips and waved them before her. She whirled on him and snatched the bag, then hugged it.

"I surrender! You satisfied?"

He brushed invisible lint off his shoulders and gave her a playful wink. "Next time you oughta have my back, chica."

"Oh, so it's like that?" she said, sashaying past him and leaving him in the aisle.

Intrigued, and not wanting to let her stray too far from his side, he quickly followed her, only to see her produce a tub of freshly made guacamole in one hand and salsa in the other. As though doing the dance of the seven veils she waved them in front of him and then spun on her heels.

"We need chips."

"Woman, you ain't right," he said, shaking his head as she fled down the aisle. "Guacamole is kryptonite—there should be limits, a truce, and an arms embargo." He looked down the aisle, concealing his concern as a man stopped and stared at him and then disappeared. Could have been nothing; they were laughing and causing a disturbance. Then again, it could have been every-thing.

"You started with the cookies and then took it to chips," she said with a casual shrug and a wide grin, bringing his attention back to her. "Your bad."

He held up both hands and conceded. It was time to get out of the store, but he had to finesse their exit. "My bad."

"Put the chips back and I'll put the guacamole back."

"Touch the guac and you lose a limb." He smiled at her.

Mia burst out laughing and then put one hand on her hip as she balanced her loot in her arms. "Go get me my cookies, then, man."

"Yes, ma'am," he said, chuckling under his breath, only too happy to accommodate any request she had. "Shame we don't have a refrigerator."

She smirked and raised an eyebrow, but said nothing. He allowed the comment to hang in the air as he hurried back to the bakery aisle. It was a great excuse to run down each aisle to see if he could spot the man who'd stopped and stared at them without tipping off Mia. At the same time, that meant leaving her for thirty seconds. But his mind relaxed when he saw the man joined in the bakery aisle with a woman and two little children.

Blowing out a long breath, he relaxed for the moment and hurriedly selected the cookies she'd requested.

Maybe the reference to their past was a little too forward. They'd had a fridge in the hotel they'd stayed at before . . . the Marriott downtown wasn't that kind of joint. But man, had they christened that room.

Still, her sexy smirk and her raised eyebrow spoke volumes. It said, *Maybe . . . maybe not.* It also said, *I remember, but I'm not speaking on it nor am I promising you anything.* He loved the mystery of not knowing for sure. But given the circumstances, that was the *last* thing he needed to be thinking about.

"What else?" he said as he met up with her, his cookie mission fulfilled.

"Gotta stay hydrated."

He just looked at her. She spun on her heels and glimpsed him over her shoulder. Dayum.

He swallowed a huge smile when she brandished a liter carton of coconut water. Roger—*that.* He hoped she meant it the way he was reading it, because buying coconut water to his way of thinking was like buying Gatorade. Electrolyte balancer in a carton. Hot damn, he could definitely go with that. Plus, she'd only grabbed one, but it was big enough to share.

With a sly smile she paused and then picked up a second carton. "You plan on working out while you're here?"

For a second he just looked at her.

"Yeah."

She nodded and put the second coconut water in the cart. "Cool. I've been trying to do more all-natural . . . this is better than stuff with artificial sweeteners and whatever."

"Yeah." He swallowed hard, suddenly finding it difficult to compose more than a syllable or two of language at a time.

"Do you want anything else?"

Again, he just stared at her for a moment. "You?"

"No, I think I'm good to go now." Mia turned away from him with a smile and then spun around. "I forgot one thing."

"What?" he said, his voice dipping to a low, mellow tone.

"Your chips! What's guac without the chips?"

"Very lonely, I suspect."

She just laughed and left him where he stood.

CHAPTER 9

Mia bit her bottom lip as she placed her items on the conveyor belt. She hadn't prepared herself for the awkward process of checking out at the supermarket. When she separated her stuff from Ryan's, he seemed slightly offended. Then there was the whole argument at the register about him paying for the full payload of grub, as he called it, even though she was trying to pay for her own stuff and neatly place her stash in one bag and his in another.

"Do not take her card," he told the confused cashier, quickly reaching around Mia to swipe his own ATM card in the machine at the register.

"But this is *my* food," Mia argued, laughing and folding her arms over her chest.

"But I asked you to come in here," Ryan countered, appearing satisfied that the transaction had gone though before she could cancel it.

"And what does *that* have to do with it?" She shook her head as his items tumbled down the belt.

"I'm old-school. I asked you, so it's assumed that I pay."

"What?"

"And when we go grab a beer, since I asked you—your money is also no good."

"Who makes up these rules?"

"The hidden brotherhood of man ways." He winked at her and chuckled as she grabbed her bag and waited for his to be packed. Then he tilted his head to the side and gave her a look. "May I ask what you're doing?"

"What?" Truly perplexed she looked around, then caught the direction of his gaze, which was on her bag. "Oh, do *not* start," she said, laughing.

"Didn't I tell you I'd be your pack mule?"

The cashier, a lanky guy in his midtwenties with wide disk piercings in his ears and wearing a tie-dyed T-shirt and jeans, gave Mia a nod. "Honey, give the man the bag. If you've got one like that, hmmmph, hmmmph, hmmmph, enjoy it, girl."

Thoroughly embarrassed, she set down the bag on the stainless-steel end of the counter. "See . . . some people just have to cause a scene."

"I don't know what you're talking about," Ryan said as he finished paying for his items and swept up both bags. "You have a nice day, and thanks," he told the cashier.

"You all have a *fabulous* afternoon, too."

Mia couldn't get out of the store fast enough. She didn't know whether to fuss or to laugh. Ryan kept stride next to her, walking on the curb side of the sidewalk, head held high, eyes forward, but his expression contained an easy, relaxed smile.

"Well, since you've commandeered my groceries and are leading this mission, General Mason, what do you feel like?"

He glanced at her with a raised brow.

"Beer or wine?" she said, clarifying, and suddenly feeling her face get warm.

"Lady's choice," he said without hesitation.

Halfway up the next block she stopped and peered in the window of a small tavern.

"What about this?" she said, glancing up at him and then reading the window menu. It was a good compromise, she hoped. "Nice wines, tempura appetizers, interesting salads and pastas, steak."

"Steak, yeah, I'm in." He peered in the window past the menu and nodded with approval. "They've got Guinness on tap. Cool."

She laughed. "Had I known that was a criteria I could have stopped a couple of blocks ago."

He didn't answer, just winked at her as he shifted both supermarket bags to one hand and then reached around her to open the door. She had to admit that there was something so nice about being treated like a lady in the smallest of ways. True, David had the social graces down to a science, but for some reason it always seemed as though he was just doing them by rote. Here, with Ryan, it felt like he was making an extra-special effort, not only because it was second nature, but because it was her. That made all the difference in the world.

As the host seated them in the nearly empty establishment, Ryan shifted his bags to one hand and pulled out her chair. The host gave him a slight smile and then moved to his chair, but Ryan thanked him and settled himself, placing the bags out of the server's path.

"I want a Merlot," Mia said, "because Chardonnay kinda gives me a headache . . . but the spicy tuna sushi looks good, but that really doesn't go with Merlot."

"Says who?" Ryan asked, leaning forward on his elbows and making a tent under his chin with his fists.

"White wines are for seafood, reds are for meats, but not poultry," she said, still deciding.

"Who said?"

She glanced up from the menu to stare at him. "People . . . I guess."

"And if you want a Merlot with your tuna sushi, will someone from the food police burst in here and confiscate your plate?"

She smiled, loving the mischief that danced in his dark brown eyes. "No . . ."

"Glad that's settled," he said, collecting her menu to set it aside.

"Yeah." She grinned, feeling almost high from the good vibes and easy interaction between them. "But can I ask you a question?"

"Depends." His smile widened as the server came over.

"Good afternoon," the gracious young woman said. "My name is Nicole, and I'll be your server. May I start you two out with a beverage?"

Ryan handed Nicole the menus after he placed their order, and when the waitress had left them, he immediately went back into his position that resembled *The Thinker* statue. "You had a question."

She did, but now she felt odd about asking it. Before the waitress had interrupted them, she'd been all ready and it would have fit into the flow. Now it seemed too intense. Plus, she'd waited for their server to leave them, which made it feel all the more foreboding.

"It was just a curiosity," Mia said, trying to make light of the question she now didn't want to ask.

"Okay . . ."

Mia laughed and shook her head. He was doing the typical blunt male thing and not making this easy for her at all. The server came back with water and delayed her question again. This time, however, Mia decided she'd come at the subject from an obtuse angle.

"I was wondering what made you finally give up the military life? You loved it so much, and . . .

I don't know. This new career path is great, but I was wondering if you ever miss what you used to do?"

Ryan hesitated and took a sip of water. He knew this question would come and he hated to lie to Mia. But there was no other option. So he hedged with a series of half-truths, hoping that would be enough.

"I guess you never fully get it out of your system," he said carefully, trying to be as evasive as possible without telling her an outright lie. "But I always said that when it was time for me to get out, I would try to do something with kids who'd been like me—on the razor's edge." That part of what he'd said was the absolute truth. It was just that his time line was very fuzzy.

"I'm really proud of you," Mia replied in a tone that ran all through him. "I said it before, but I really think what you're doing is great." She leaned forward and rested her elbows on the table, staring at him. "And nobody scooped you up and took you off the market in all these years?"

Wow . . . that was *not* the next line of questioning he'd expected. He thought she was going down the career path, but this was a blind ambush. Suddenly self-conscious, he just laughed.

"Nah . . . my lifestyle was pretty chaotic in the military. It was hard on relationships." He moved back to allow the waitress to set down their drinks, thankful that he'd have a beer in his hand while undergoing this line of interrogation. "I didn't meet anybody I could bring home to Momma," he said with a smile, taking a deep swig of the dark ale.

"You really didn't meet anybody in all that time?" Mia murmured and then looked up with a challenging smirk.

He set down his beer and placed both hands flat on the table. "I was stationed in some pretty exotic places around the world. They have you on the move all the time . . . in and out of foreign countries or battle theaters that can get a woman stoned to death if she speaks to you—infidel that you are . . ." Their waitress Nicole brought their food as he spoke, and he bit into his spicy chicken. "When I get married, I want to do it once and for final . . . have a couple of kids and be best friends with my wife. You don't get to be best friends with a booty call that you met online or in a bar in Brazil, you know what I mean?"

Mia nodded and picked up her sushi with a delicate flourish of chopsticks, now fully recovered. "I hadn't thought of it that way."

"Neither had I, truth be told, until I started living it."

"That must have been hard . . ." Her voice trailed off with a gentle sigh, but there was still a little mischief playing around the edges of her lovely mouth.

"That's one way of looking at it. But you get used to not having certain things in your life." Ryan smiled even though Mia seemed to be momentarily rendered speechless. That was both a good thing and a bad thing, because it gave him too much time to think.

As a diversion, Ryan bit into a loaded potato skin, pretending for a moment to be absorbed in his plate, while wondering how this woman was able to strip him bare with just a question and a smile. But she made him want to tell her things he'd never even contemplated putting into words. Until now, those things were just a quiet sense that something was missing in his life, and he'd shove whatever that something was into the back of his mind, always focusing on a mission that took precedence. The problem was, she'd somehow become his mission, and he knew full well that he had to get back to the prime directive after this brief interlude.

"You know I don't even know what to say to that." Mia popped a piece of sushi into her mouth and began chewing, but her eyes smiled until there were tiny crinkles at the outer corners.

"What?" he said with a lopsided smile, still chewing. "Me saying that you get used to not having certain things in your life?"

"Yeah, but really? It's just that easy?"

"You get used to no running water, mosquitoes the size of a quarter. There's a lot you get used to . . . but I think I fared better than guys who were married and had somebody back home waiting on them. It's like that *You don't miss what you don't have* thing."

"Oh . . ."

He watched her expression cloud over and knew he had to double back and make a correction. He was *not* talking about her; he was talking about the state of being single in the military. But he knew enough to know that most women didn't speak in broad strokes. Everything was personal.

"It took a while to get used to being on my own again," he said quietly, holding her gaze for a moment. "I don't want you to think there was anything easy about that at all. But they give you stuff to do in the military till your ass is so bone-weary and run so ragged, you become philosophical."

"Philosophical," she said, her gorgeous smile returning.

Ryan watched the restaurant begin to fill with the after-work crowd and just shrugged. "Yeah. Things like not having toilet paper in the jungle make you philosophical. Not having anywhere dry to sleep—yeah, that makes you philosophical. Somewhere between Panama and Afghanistan, two extremes in climate by the way, I became philosophical. Then there are places like Korea, the Philippines, and Amsterdam that have so many excesses you also become philosophical from that."

Mia nodded. "Tell me you're not selling Amsterdam as a place that breeds sudden philosophy . . . but I can see how no toilet paper in the jungle would make you philosophical."

"That's all I'm saying." He bit into another wing, glad that her good mood had returned. "And, yes, severe excess can also cause a man to become philosophical." When Mia drew back with a smile and a frown, he pressed on, thoroughly enjoying their sparring match. "There were certain things I could delete from my mental file that others who weren't solo couldn't. If you have kids, you're gonna stress around birthdays and Christmas. If you have a sweetheart, an anniversary or whatever is gonna make you blue. But me, I became philosophical."

"And nothing about home upset you while you were gone?"

"As long as I knew you were okay and my mom was all right, I was good." He hesitated, took a deep swig from his beer, determined to close her investigation with authority as the tables and bar around them began to fill up with patrons. "But since there were no cherry blossoms in the Middle East, I was good to go."

"Oh . . . ," she murmured, seeming pleased and sated with the information he'd given her.

Rather than dwell on the hollow spaces in his soul, humor was the best way he knew of to diffuse the deep-feelings bomb that only Mia could set off. With a few memories linked to key words and phrases, a smile, and a well-timed sigh, it was as though he'd tripped over an emotional IED. Everything about Mia was an improvised explosive device. Hell, he was still carrying shrapnel from the first time they were together.

"So, this dude that's at the conference . . . am I going to have to show him some old-school hand-to-hand, or you think he'll be cool?" Ryan took another sip of his beer. It was time to get the focus off his life and onto hers.

"No. Like I told you earlier, he's arrogant but not a problem like that."

"Okay, because you know . . ."

Mia smiled. "I *do* know."

"Because I can come into your presentation with my boys and we can holler and give you a standing ovation if he's in there—and boo him, if he's presenting."

"Oh, God, whatever you do, please don't do that . . . and he's not presenting anyway." Mia covered her face with both hands, laughing.

"So now you're philosophical . . . where you see someone you've been with, the interaction is over, and what they say or think no longer matters. You're immovable. It rolls off your back. That's becoming philosophical."

"Oh, then when it comes to him, call me Socrates."

Now he had to laugh. "Damn, that's cold. Why are women always so cold?"

"I'm just saying."

"No twinge, no spark?"

"Puhlease." Mia waved a hand at him and went back to her sushi. "Like you just said, you don't miss what you never had."

He just stared at Mia while she ate. Her casually

delivered statement was so loaded that he was afraid to touch it. But curiosity made him poke at the edge of it to see if it was live ammo and ticking.

"Never missed what you never had?" Ryan arched an eyebrow and polished off his last potato skin. "That's a deep way to describe a relationship."

"Not really," she said with a wry twist of her mouth. "If you finally accept that you never had true passion, a real connection, or genuine respect between you and a specific person, then you have to admit that you really can't miss what you've never had with them."

"Yeah," he murmured, and then hailed their waitress and sent his gaze toward the window.

Each person who came to the front of the establishment gave him pause. Mia's name had been mentioned in deadly chatter, and while sitting with her, he knew he was more dangerous than any terrorist could ever hope to be if they tried to hurt her. Yet he couldn't upset her or tip her off by seeming paranoid. Every shadowy character who stopped to read the posted menu made him want to draw a weapon—and at the same time he knew that was absurd. He was clearly losing focus, had to get back on track.

But what Mia had said was the stone-cold truth, and it echoed through the secret hollow inside him that he'd promised himself he'd ignore. There was definitely no being philosophical or disciplined around her. There was only one thing to do. Agree with her and order another round of beer and Merlot.

CHAPTER 10

Mia accepted a fresh glass of Merlot from the waitress and then glanced around at the growing crowd. Even as she took a casual sip, everything within her screamed that another glass of wine was a bad idea.

First of all, if the little establishment they'd found was now loaded with people, it meant that attendees from the conference had finally left the hotel to overflow to surrounding area restaurants. That meant it was getting late. That meant she should have been back in her room prepping for her big debut, not getting über-relaxed and basking in the wonderful conversational flow of one Ryan Mason.

Second of all, she had to remember that, even though Dr. Cortland wasn't an uptight old bird, she was still here as a professional and this conference was a part of her job. She had to keep her behavior above reproach. She had to stop feeling the charisma oozing off the best lover she'd ever known . . . had to shut that part of her brain down. Damn, Ryan Mason's timing sucked.

"But you know what really messed me up while I was away?" he said, seeming as though he was studying the suds in his glass. "The thing I couldn't get philosophical about?"

"No, what?" she said quietly, her voice almost drowned out by the restaurant din.

"Spanish Harlem." He offered her a sad smile that they both knew went way deeper than he'd ever admit.

"Ah . . . el barrio." She nodded and took a deeper sip of wine.

"Where was that joint you took me to . . . up on like 116th Street between Lexington and Third. Oh, man, those fried rinds . . . ridiculous."

"You mean the cuchifritos," she said laughing.

"Yeah, those." He shook his head. "Then that place on 116th and Camaradas near 114th with the sangria and avocado dip that will make you wanna slap yo' Momma." Ryan used her laughter as a diversion as he scoped a patron who'd taken a seat at the bar. The man's stare lingered five seconds too long.

"Don't forget the live bands—Bomba y Plena, sí?"

"Okay, Mia, don't start talking sexy to me after ten years. Have a heart." Again he kept the banter going, dividing his focus between her and the man in the shadows nursing a beer.

She laughed, seeming embarrassed but flattered.

"You started it with going back to el barrio, hombre. No mas por favor, and it's all good."

"See, there you go." He lifted his glass with a wide grin, glanced at the bar from the corner of his eye, and then looked at her. "I'm gonna have to go to one of those joints and get a cure if you don't knock it off."

"Me?" she exclaimed, and placed a hand over her heart laughing. "You cannot blame me if you decide to go into a botanica. But for your information, La Otti, up on 116th and Park, specializes in love potions . . . so I might have to go get a candle on you, if you don't stop messing with me."

"Oh, now I see what's happened here. I'm the victim of a long-term potion." He winked at her and sipped his beer, taking a deep gulp before he set his glass down. He caught the eye of the man at the bar. It was an instant exchange, but once it occurred the man got up, paid his tab, and slipped out the door. "But maybe it was that place on 106th that did me in years ago."

"La Fonda . . . ," she cooed, remembering that dinner and the subject matter they were dancing around without speaking on. After great food there was always mind-bending sex. But for the sake of conversation, she kept her mentions strictly about the food.

"Yeah . . . ," he said in a deep murmur. *"That place."* He was going to have to kill a bastard tonight.

"True, authentic pernil and arroz con guandules."

"See . . . there you go again," he teased, but his smile was mellower and he was leaning forward.

"My bad. Roast pork and rice and peas," she said with a slow smile, clarifying in a way that she hoped took him back to the same date she remembered. "With jukebox salsa and merengue music . . . and coquito yum, otherwise known as coconut rum punch."

He nodded and didn't answer her for a moment. "Kinda hard to become philosophical about that."

At a temporary loss for words as his mood shifted from playful to intense, she just nodded and sipped her wine.

"Just as hard as I suppose it would be to become philosophical about spending all day chilling in Prospect Park or skating at the Empire Rink . . . or ending up at Akwaaba Mansion."

Ryan downed his beer. "I wasn't going to mention that bed-and-breakfast."

She shrugged. "Just saying."

He nodded. "I missed you."

"Same here." She finished her wine and released a slow sigh. "It feels like yesterday . . . then a part of me is like . . . wait, Mia, ten years has gone by and suddenly this feels real intense and confusing." She laughed at herself. "Maybe the second glass of wine was a bad idea, huh?"

"Or maybe this whole situation *is* intense and

confusing and there's nothing wrong with your instincts."

When she couldn't meet Ryan's gaze, he covered her hand with his for a moment and just looked at her until she stared at him.

"Let me cut to the chase, Mia. I know you're here for your job and so am I. But I do want to reconnect—even if just having a little time right now is all it can be until the conference is over. There are a lot of gaps to fill in, and I know you'd need to ask me a bunch more questions over time . . . like I don't expect to just parachute into your life in a hotel lobby and for you to act like a decade hasn't passed."

"Well, I'm glad we got that out of the way," she said with a self-conscious chuckle. When she released her breath and relaxed, the warmth of his easy smile coated her insides.

"I've kicked myself a thousand times for ever letting you go," he said, his smile fading. "That's what really made me philosophical. After a while you either live with regrets or try to force yourself to go on. Part of that is the lie you tell yourself about how things weren't meant to be, yada, yada, yada. How it probably wouldn't have worked. That's where you become the philosopher and then nothing after that seems as intense or as passionate or . . . worth the trouble, you know what I mean?"

"Yeah," she said, toying with the stem of her glass. "I know a little something about that."

"But I can't lie and say I'm not glad you aren't married or living with somebody. Just like I can't lie that hearing you bounce between Spanish and English doesn't mess me up on a level that we're not going to discuss right now."

He drew back and hailed the waitress, leaving the burn of his touch to simmer on the back of her hand. Mia breathed very slowly, watching Ryan's serious, stone-carved profile. The last thing in the world she'd expected was for him to reenter her life and then to sock her right between the eyes with the truth.

There was no doubt the man wanted her, but he'd also said as plain as day that he wouldn't crowd her. Just like their first time around . . . But this time she was all grown up, remembered every detail of what it felt like to be in his arms, and wasn't sure she didn't want to be crowded.

"Can I get you anything else?" their waitress asked, snapping Mia out of her daze.

"Merlot . . . coffee, dessert?" Ryan said in a low rumble and staring at Mia in a way that she could feel between her legs.

"Nothing for me, thank you," Mia managed to reply.

"You, sir?"

Ryan just shook his head. "No, thank you. Just the check, please."

"I'll be right back with that," their waitress said, then gave them both a sly smile before she slipped away.

"I'd better prep for tomorrow," Mia said, trying to reset the mood to establish more distance.

"Yeah . . . makes sense," Ryan replied, but his intense gaze said otherwise.

"I really appreciate the groceries and dinner . . . and the wonderful company," she said, just above a whisper, staring at his mouth.

"I appreciate that you even allowed this," he said, the rumble of his voice now creating goose-flesh on her arms.

"Why wouldn't I have?" she asked, dangerously edging near the subject that should have been left abandoned for the night.

"Because I was a damned fool and didn't fight for what was really important to me. Fought for everything else, but not this . . . won't happen again."

"It takes two. It happened on both our watch."

Mia began picking at the edge of the tablecloth. There was no safe haven for her gaze, her hands, or her thoughts. Suddenly the little oasis of a restaurant they'd found felt too crowded and left her nerves raw. From out of nowhere she felt moisture fill her eyes, and she could hear her voice getting shaky. What did you say to a man you'd loved with all your heart and soul, but whom you thought was gone forever? And how did you begin a conversation with that man—a conversation that required profound truth about how you felt—in an era that taught people to guard their emotions and to not seem too needy. But she needed him now so badly that it was almost impossible to speak.

Ryan studied the shimmer in Mia's eyes, watched her swallow hard, and took in the slight warble in her voice. The fact that she was battling such strong emotions normally would have put him on his feet to round the table and draw her into his arms, but he'd never disrespect her in a crowded establishment that might have colleagues lurking.

Instead he watched her take a deep breath and steady herself. His gaze caressed the smooth contour of her face, down her delicate throat, noticing how the quiet intensity between them had pebbled her flesh . . . making her nipples peak beneath her tank top. He looked away with a hard swallow, searching for their waitress to pay the bill—any distraction that would kill the ache in his groin.

"I didn't fight hard enough, either," Mia finally said, her voice steadier now, but husky and quiet. "At that age, you always think there's time . . . always think . . ."

He covered her hand again, unable to resist touching her. "You always think there's time," he repeated, trying to convey that he understood more than she knew. "And then comes the day when you realize time is finite."

She turned her palm over so that the soft center

submitted to his. "Sí, mi tesoro. We both share la filosofía."

He simply nodded, now focused on her touch, remembering the satin-smooth inside of her palm with cellular memory hard enough to cause a slight shudder.

"Thank you," their waitress said, interrupting every carnal thought in his head. "I'll take that whenever you're ready."

The break was good; the air did him even better. How things had gotten so crazy so quickly, he couldn't have explained if his life depended on it. But the short walk back to the hotel gave him only temporary respite. Mia's silence and nearness just seemed to make desire settle between them like a squatter, refusing to budge, refusing to give ground, until he just gave up and threaded his arm around her waist.

It had felt like such a natural thing to do that muscle memory had propelled his limb forward on its own as they crossed the street and walked beneath the dark area of scaffolding a block away from the hotel. But what he wasn't prepared for was for her to stiffen at his touch, and he immediately fell back with an apology lodged in his throat—then noticed why she'd frozen on him.

The asshole was back, and walking in their direction. He was with three of his friends. Ryan did a fast assessment. They'd come out of O'Hara's, the watering hole across the street. From the look in the guy's eyes, not only did he have three buddies with him, but he was also three sheets to the wind.

"So, we meet again," David called out to Mia, shaking his head and laughing. But his eyes were hard, flashing fire.

"Man, let it go," one of his friends said, trying to grab his arm, but David flung off his friend's hold.

"Come on," Mia said, her voice low and frightened. "Let's cross the street. I don't want any trouble—he gets really ugly when he's drunk."

"I don't think so," Ryan said, squaring his shoulders and making sure Mia was well behind him. He looked at the three buddies. They weren't a problem; they'd only been out for a few beers and maybe to listen to a steinful of David's bullshit. But David was snot-slinging drunk, had obviously seen his arm around Mia, and had spotted bags from the supermarket. Street basics told Ryan that this was a man ready to do something stupid.

"Why don't you let the lady pass and be cool, man?" Ryan kept his voice neutral and logical as David got closer.

"Lady?" David scoffed and then looked at the supermarket bags. "If you say so."

Ryan moved Mia to his opposite side with a gentle hand at her back. "Come on. I'm not dignifying that. You're drunk."

"Not here," one of David's friends whined. "Let's not get into anything crazy, okay."

"Listen to your boys," Ryan warned as David continued to move in his and Mia's direction. Mia's ex had no idea how tightly wound he was after getting the encrypted text and seeing that someone was possibly tailing her. "I am not the one. Not tonight. Trust me, brother."

"Fuck you—stay out of it," David said, slurring his words. "This is between me and my bitch fiancée."

"Whoa, whoa, whoa. Fall back. *Now*." The urge to glance back at Mia for corroboration that she'd been engaged to this asshole was nearly as strong as the urge to drop the fool before him, but Ryan held his ground.

"What!" Mia shouted, responding to David's taunt and clearing Ryan's side. Her accent had sharpened and every ounce of el barrio was back in her tone. Her index finger swayed in the air to the beat of her argument as a hand moved firmly to her hip. "First of all, I am so not your fiancée that it isn't even funny. Second of all, why are you out here causing a scene and acting like a complete idiot? It's over, been over, and you need to go get a cup of coffee and sober up!"

David's three friends were now noticeably behind him, each looking like a deer caught in the headlights of a Mack truck.

"Come on, David," another of them said. "Don't call her names . . . it's not cool."

Ryan again moved Mia to his inside so they could pass, all the while watching a red-faced David yank away from the tentative tug of his friend. But from the corner of his eye, he saw it happen in slow motion. Mia glared at David as they passed him; something within David snapped and made him reach out to pull Mia's arm; then Ryan felt something fragile within him snap. It was a chain reaction. Sheer instinct propelled him in a reverse spin to catch David in the jaw with his elbow—and it was only for the sake of Mia that he pulled the blow. Instantly, David went down, but he wasn't out, just stunned. David's three friends backed up, and then finally one went to his aid.

"Put your hands on her again, and the next time you'll have to get your jaw wired. Call her something other than her name again, and I swear you'll need to see a dental surgeon." Ryan adjusted the bags in his hands and stared at Mia. "Let's go."

Mia hesitated and then followed the command to move out. Adrenaline was spiking in his system so hard that his ears were ringing. He said nothing as she rummaged in her pocket to get the hotel key out so they could enter through the back security door. It was dark, the street was deserted—this was how women got jacked. The key should have already been in her hand.

Ryan kept his gaze scanning, half praying that David would get up and give him a reason to truly kick his ass. The real bastard he wanted was the one who had entered the restaurant to follow Mia, and anybody else who'd uttered her name on a cell phone transmission.

David wisely decided to go stand with his friends when he was able to get up, rubbing his jaw. Ryan nodded at David. It was an old-fashioned curt acknowledgment from the streets that meant the next time there would be blood. He didn't care if David knew the code or not. It was a promise conveyed in a steely grit and a pulsing jaw. Ryan returned his attention to Mia. Her hands were shaking as she finally got out her key.

Mia swiped her key card and quickly opened the glass hotel door, then gave him a pleading look to drop it. He made no commitment, just followed her into the building.

They didn't speak as they walked down the long corridor to the lobby, passing conference attendees and standing groups of professors. They stood side by side quietly and waited for the laboriously slow elevator to arrive, and remained silent on the way up to Mia's floor.

"He's not done, you know that, right?" Ryan muttered as they neared her room.

"But I am. Damn it. I am so sorry you had to deal with that," she said, her eyes blazing with anger. "He had no right, and if you hadn't tagged him I would have." Mia spun around and leaned against her door with her eyes closed and ruffled her fingers through her hair. "Oh! I swear I cannot stand him!"

"Open the door and put your bag in your room," Ryan said in a firm tone, then dropped his voice. "You don't know who has a room on this hallway and this isn't something you want getting around in your professional circles, right?"

Mia nodded. "You're right," she said more quietly. "Thank you."

He waited until she opened her door and then handed Mia her groceries. "If you need an escort in the morning, let me know. Like I said, he's pissed, been embarrassed . . . and obviously isn't rational. This is how women get hurt, so don't underestimate that bastard. Understood?"

"Yeah," she said, accepting the grocery bag. "But I really am sorry you had to see that."

"No problem," Ryan replied with a shrug, still feeling the aftereffects of an adrenaline rush. He would be sure to stay on her flank given everything going on—especially the things she had no way to know about. Rather than totally panic her, he focused his concern onto her ex—something tangible that might make her take precautions. "Just remember, this guy was invested . . . a fiancé. It's not the same thing as a jealous boyfriend. This takes it up a notch. So you watch your back and call me, even if you just feel nervous—all right?"

She turned and pushed the door open farther, but

oddly took up his free hand. "I want to tell you something, okay? It's not for the hall, like you said."

He didn't resist or ask for clarification as she pulled him over the threshold and gently shut the door behind him. He set down his bag at his feet and she set down hers. But he waited, not sure where this was going.

"I didn't want you to find out that I had been engaged like that," she said looking down at the bags. "It wasn't an emotional investment, like you think, either. It was messy . . . twisted. I just wanted you to know that."

He placed one finger under her chin and lifted her face so she would look at him. "You don't owe me any explanation for whatever was going on in your life. Seriously."

"I know . . . but after the great afternoon we shared and how everything felt so open and honest between us, then here this situation comes out of a dark alley to blindside us."

He couldn't let her stand there and think he was completely devoid of secrets, but he wasn't at liberty to divulge them. All he knew to do was to trace her cheek and hope that she could feel how much he'd missed her through that lingering touch.

"Mia . . . we've had lives in between the time we shared. I know that. I guess half of what pissed me off about him getting in your face was that I hated how he'd addressed you, and down deep I wish I'd been the one to put a ring on your finger first."

Ryan closed his eyes, suddenly realizing just how much he hated that she'd almost married another man. But a soft kiss melted that resentment away. The light taste of Merlot and ginger fused with Angel perfume and the softest lips dredged his soul of male combat, and then replaced it with something more basic.

Tight muscles in his shoulders unwound as she leaned up and he bent to deepen their kiss, his arms enfolding her, muscle memory taking over. She fit into the same sacred space that no one else had ever been able to occupy. Her tongue owned his, gently dueling with it in a slow, sultry dance, a rumba that caused his eyes to cross beneath his lids. His hands sought her hair as her curvaceous frame fit against his, molding the she-softness of woman against the he-hardness of man, making him forget that he was on duty, off post, and way over the line.

"There's been nobody like you," she murmured into his mouth as she broke their kiss. Her fingers trembled as they stroked his jaw. "I missed you so much that it hurts now just to look at you."

This time when he took her mouth it was a hard crush. Unable to tell her, he could only show her, tearing his mouth away from hers to kiss her eyelids, the bridge of her nose, and then spilled kisses down her throat. Her hair felt so good that it made his hands ache, and as she ground her pelvis against him, the only sound he could release was a deep, midchest moan.

Bare-skin shoulders beckoned his lips, then palms; her soft sighs and gasps encouragement to take the hill, plant a flag, and claim her territory as her body literally surrendered to his. He caught her in the sway of her back, paid homage to her breastbone and lifted her, stepped over bags, navigating around luggage to find the bed. He'd set her down gently, but she'd pulled him roughly to blanket her. The position was like a flash point for both of them as she arched beneath him and wrapped her legs around his waist.

Need put tears in his eyes. Memory put her hands at his back to fist his shirt. That sent his palms beneath the glorious swell of her perfect ass. Caught up in the momentum of passion, he was soon thrusting as if he were in deep, wincing because he wasn't, but unable for several seconds to stop.

Jesus help him, it had been so long. The jeans were shredding his sanity, her soft whimpers driving him to find a way to please her.

Remembering the contours of her body in the blind, his hands rounded the tight lobes of her backside to sweep over the swell of her hips. Fabric textures changed and soon her tank top gave way to bare torso.

Ryan pulled back . . . some things were so sacred that you had to stop in reverence. Mia's body was that. Distant city lights spilled into the window with the moon, dappling over her satin skin. He watched her yank her tank top over her head and held his breath as she unhooked the front of her bra, but left it for him to peel off her.

Gently, he opened the lacy cups and allowed her breasts to bounce free. She closed her eyes as though the air alone tortured the sensitive skin. For a moment he couldn't move; the beauty of what lay before him was almost surreal. Just as he'd remembered, her large quarter-size nipples were the color of caramel, a shade darker than her skin, and stood erect taunting him, begging him to suckle them. Had she any idea how many nights he'd remembered them, alone, quietly relieving the pain of missing her with quick, agonized strokes?

He bent to kiss the tender undersides of the swollen lobes, and then watched her bring a fist to her mouth to stifle a moan. Slow licks against the tight skin made her belly tremble, his cheek grazing their surface, his hands gently palming them so his lips could pull both nipples to meet his eager tongue. But where was her voice, her glorious, deep-throated voice . . . that sound that replayed in his mind around the world on every lonely night he had endured?

Determined to find it, he slid down her body and helped her out of her jeans, resting his burning cheek against her belly, fearing his heart might give out once he tasted her again.

Silk panties, peach; her skin caramel. Legs equally silky in texture . . . long, smooth, and opened for him as he slid away her underwear to settle his gaze on the silky triangle of dark hair between her thighs.

"I'm sorry," she murmured, and then tried to pull away from him.

He didn't understand. "Baby . . . what's wrong?"

"I didn't shave, I didn't expect . . ."

His kiss between her thighs drowned out her complaint as he gently pulled her body closer to him by the nook behind her knees. Was she crazy? He was home. Everything he'd remembered, everything he'd missed he tried to tell her with the tip of his tongue and the pulse of his suckles. French kisses and two-fingered pressure lifted her backside off the duvet and began to salsa her hips, turning her quick pants into long moaned wind chants. He found her voice; resurrected it from the dead. It got hollered into a pillow when she spilled sweet coquito yum nectar down his chin.

Panting, winded, and covered with a slight sheen of perspiration that made her skin glisten in the moonlight, she half opened her eyes and gazed at him from beneath heavy lids.

She was so beautiful like that, naked, legs spread, hair tousled, his fingers slowly sliding in and out of her slickness . . . her hips slowly undulating as her body trembled from small ripples of after-pleasure. His groin hurt so badly now that he had to breathe through his mouth.

"Put it in just a little bit, papi?" she murmured and then reached for him.

"I can't . . . I'll come before I'm halfway in," he admitted in a deep rasp. "I don't have anything on me."

"Me either." She sat up and bent toward him, holding his face between her warm hands, and then kissed him deeply. "I wasn't expecting this, but it's still your turn."

Ryan closed his eyes tightly as her hands found his jean fastenings, but he had to help her get the zipper down and work around the unyielding bulge without hurting him. The moment his pants were down and he was freed, he collapsed against her.

"Oh, God, Mia, I missed you so much." His words spilled into her hair as thick pre-cum spilled over her soft hands when they sheathed him.

Sound and sensation collided, sending torque though his spine as the wet-slick sound of her strokes fused with the soft heat of her palms. Mia's sweet scent branded his nose; her naked breasts filled his hands. All of it sent snap-jerk thrusts into her palms, but when she bent to take him into her mouth, his voice exploded in a low, subsonic moan.

The warmth of her mouth, the tease of her tongue, almost made him throw her down on the bed to take her up on her offer. *Put it in just a little bit, papi,* haunted his mind, while he prayed that her gag reflex would hold out. Slim hands soon replaced her mouth as she suckled his sac, her breasts grazing his shaft as she leaned up to take him again. But he held her shoulders. The convulsion was so near that he couldn't take another change, another interruption as his head dropped back, every cord of muscle in his body tensed, and the spasm hit him so hard that it felt like he'd seized.

It seemed like half an hour had passed before he could move, but the rational part of his brain told him that it had only been a few minutes. He'd spilled down her breasts and her hands, and she still caressed him with the warm fluid.

"You okay?" she murmured, looking up at him.

He nodded, still catching his breath. "Yeah . . . you?"

She smiled. "Watching you get off so intensely sorta got me going again . . . but I'll live."

He leaned down and kissed her soft mouth. "That's how we'd always wind up in our neverending sessions."

"I know . . . but I do have to get up in the morning to give a presentation." She laughed softly. "And I had like fifty questions to ask you . . . this wasn't supposed to happen, you parachuting into my life and then boom."

"Delta Force, that's what we do." He smiled, still catching his breath.

"Delta Force?" She tilted her head, questioning him.

"I meant—"

"You really missed me? Because Madre d'Dios, Ryan, I missed you so badly."

"Mia . . . I can't even explain what losing you was like." All the playfulness had gone out of his tone as he studied her sad expression. He held her face between his palms, closing his eyes as she stroked his still-hard member. "Oh, baby . . . you have no idea what I would give just to stay all night with you . . . no worries, nobody to have to answer to . . . no pretense." He let out a hard sigh, remembering what it was like to fit against her naked backside like a spoon, a perfect fit, and able to enter her half in his sleep.

"One day soon," she said, taking his mouth.

"One day soon," he promised, kissing her hard.

"I want to feel you inside me . . ."

He groaned and leaned his forehead against hers. "Mia . . . give a workingman a break."

She laughed softly and nipped his ear. "When you go to your room, I'm going to take a shower, then get in bed and spread my legs, thinking of you, smelling you in my sheets . . . then I'm going to slip a finger inside and make believe it's you."

He shuddered, and although it made her laugh, it was no act. "I'll probably be up all night going through bottles of hotel lotion, panting your name . . . come on, girl . . . stop before it starts all over again."

Kissing her hard, he extracted himself from her hold and tried to gather up his pants. "Mind if I wash up a little? I mean, just in case I accidentally bump into somebody in the hall."

"Sure . . . you can take a shower, if you want."

He just stared at her.

"Okay, maybe not," she said laughing. "Or we won't get to sleep tonight."

He nodded and backed away from the bed with a grimace. "My point exactly."

"Call me?"

"Tonight?"

"Yeah . . . ," she said, rolling over on her stomach and looking up at him with a sexy smile.

His BlackBerry was being monitored; the airwaves were being tracked for potential cell phone irregularities and potential terrorist chatter. Phone sex was the last thing he could do with her here. This was bad enough.

"No, Mia. Absolutely not. You have a presentation in the morning, and, uh, one round of phone sex and I'll be at an all-night pharmacy buying a twelve-pack, then keeping you up till dawn."

Mia rolled over on her back and giggled like a schoolgirl. "That was the plan, but I guess you're right. I'll behave if you say so."

"Good . . . because tonight, I say so."

CHAPTER 11

He stood by the door, a dark silhouette, fisting her hair and crushing her mouth with his . . . smelling like fresh soap, a solid wall of maleness that stole her breath. She'd said things to him that shamed her, had opened herself up and made herself vulnerable, but in the context of having lost him before, that meant nothing. And, yet, now standing naked by the door with Ryan about to leave, she felt like a complete fool. Worse than that, she felt like all those things her ex had called her . . . anything but a lady. There were questions she should have asked before any of this happened; barriers she should have erected, but, God, please tell her how.

All of a sudden, every lonely hour, every tear cried had manifested in a second chance and she'd thrown caution and common sense to the wind.

Her tears mingled with the trace of toothpaste in

his mouth, making their minted kiss salty, making him hold her tighter, tight enough to make her want to sob.

"I'm scared," she admitted in a thick whisper against his chest.

"I swear to God I'm not going to hurt you, Mia," he murmured in a warm rush against the crown of her head.

Trembling with the need for him and the fear of what he could do to her heart, she stared up at him, no longer censuring the tears that streamed down her cheeks.

"Why didn't you come for me, fight for me . . . say that you couldn't live without me the way I couldn't live without you—because I've been dead since you've been gone. It was so fast and so unfair, Ryan . . . I didn't know where you were. I didn't know when you'd be coming home. I didn't even have a damned address! What was I supposed to do?" Her hands became fists against his stone-carved chest, and then fell away as a sob choked off her words. "What was I supposed to do?" she whispered into the fabric of his shirt as his arms enfolded her.

He hung his head, his forehead now resting on hers, his deep, pain-filled breaths giving her the courage to press on. It was clear that he didn't know the answer to her question any more than she did.

"And I promised myself I would never go here, wouldn't cry, wouldn't trip . . . and you've made me lie to myself," she said, squeezing her eyes shut tightly and holding him as closely as he held her. "When I saw you in the lobby and you said let's go hang for a beer, I swore I could handle that and could keep it casual . . . thought I was strong enough after all this time to go in with my guard up—said that I was going to take my time, and take it slow, and make sense, and not lead with my heart or my body but with my head, and look at this shit that just happened."

"I don't even know where to begin," he murmured. "Every charge against me is true . . . and there's still a lot I need to tell you one day, but if you don't believe anything I've ever said to you, believe this—there has never been anybody that's made me feel this way." He drew in a deep breath, inhaling her and shaking his head. "You don't think I'm scared? This wasn't supposed to happen, to go this far. I thought I had distance enough to start with a fresh slate, begin at a new beginning . . . but it picked up exactly where we left off and I'm way beyond caught up, too."

"So now what?" she whispered, staring up at him.

His lips brushed her face, kissing away tears, his fingers trembling as they followed the curve of her cheek in the dark.

"Mia, all I can promise you is that I'm not playing with your mind or your heart . . . and I have to ask you to trust me. I have no right to . . . but baby, please just give me a little latitude and it'll be all right."

"You're married," she whispered, pulling back, her voice filled with so much disappointment that it sounded flat even to her own ears.

"No," he said, holding her by her upper arms and staring at her in the shadows. "I have some career issues, but it's not a woman or a wife, all right?"

Slowly she nodded and relaxed. Slowly he released his grip on her arms and then closed his eyes.

"This got intense and confusing, like you said earlier," she murmured.

He nodded. "It may be intense but I'm not confused about what I want." He stared at her, his gaze so deep in the swath of moonlight that she almost looked away from him. "Are you?"

"No," she murmured.

He lightly rubbed his thumb over her mouth as though afraid to kiss her again. "I'm going to go—because I have to. You are going to get some rest—because you have to. And I'll see you, front row, in the morning."

"Okay . . ." She touched his mouth with the tip of her finger, sealing the last kiss he'd given her in with it.

He lifted his chin, opened the door, and slipped through it, allowing it to close behind him with a soft click.

He walked down the hall with force. He had to get outside. Needed space. Couldn't wait for a slow elevator. Had to get his head together. Mia made every cell in his body hurt. His phone was now vibrating off his hip. He prayed she hadn't sent him a sweet nothing or worse, a sext pic that would become a permanent part of an intelligence database. She was for his eyes only . . . his confidential report. His need-to-know basis.

But the two word text from Ken recalibrated his mind and his body: *Code red.*

In a flat-out dash, Ryan headed toward the exit at the end of the hall and hit the door, barreling down the steps. Ken was on the landing below him and simply slapped an M1911 in his hand as they continued spiraling down the staircase. Noticing that Ken's weapon was concealed, he slipped his under his shirt in the back waistband of his pants.

"Sitrep."

"Intelligence intercepted an email transmission of a lone wolf in Connecticut. We've got a vehicle outside, Captain. Indications are that he's gonna make a move tomorrow."

"Location?"

"We don't know—his email wasn't specific, just a big splash in the Big Apple. Feds had him in their sights and he slipped them. Then we got a cell phone tweet that he was on his way in to Manhattan."

They crossed the lobby shoulder-to-shoulder, passing hotel patrons and staff with authority. Ken gave a quick lift of his chin to indicate the black GMC with the motor running. Then Ethan was behind the wheel and pulled off as soon as Ken and Ryan jumped in and slammed their doors.

"Just got a feed that the feds closed in on an abandoned vehicle in Times Square," Ethan said over his shoulder. "It had been sitting there all afternoon, Cap—but when it started smoking, vendors alerted local police. It had really amateur bomb-making components in it that didn't detonate. Can you believe we're just getting this intel up the food chain almost six hours later?"

"That is complete bullshit, but I believe it," Ryan said, his gaze straight ahead. "And we're just now getting this info?"

"Affirmative, Captain."

Her hair was still damp when she awakened. Fatigue and the need to cocoon in bed for a few hours to recover won out over the vanity of blow-drying after a shampoo and a hot shower. Her heart was raw, just like her nerves, as she stared at the blue-gray filter of dawn haunting her window. But she had to get up. No matter what, she had a job to do this morning, and it wasn't about throwing away Dr. Cortland's belief in her. Wasn't about throwing away an entire career because of a personal meltdown the night before.

Mia got up and focused. She went to the closet and found her blue suit, and then her pearls and her low-heeled pumps, slowly gathering her uniform as she softly said her presentation aloud to absolutely no one in her room.

Ryan stood on the other side of the interrogation glass in the Federal Building with his arms folded over his chest, refusing to look to his watch. Today the media was going to have a field day with news of the thwarted Times Square bombing attempt, but this was just one of a growing number of self-inspired madmen—a guy with no direct ties to the main plot he and his unit were tracking.

And yet this bastard and his little band of fertilizer funders had taken him away from protecting the hotel on a wild goose chase. Feds were supposed to be their backup, covering the hotel while he and his special detachment got to the threat and extracted intel before Miranda rights had to be read.

The big problem was that, even though this guy's plot had failed because his homemade bomb lessons off the Internet had failed to sharpen his skills, one day there'd be someone who would be able to pull of what this guy had tried. Tracking down every threat, investigating every lead drained valuable resources. Who knew which ones were the real deal until you took them all down? Who knew when a true threat was going to surface? Ryan steadied himself and prepared for the long haul. It was like playing fucking Whac-A-Mole at an amusement park.

*   *   *

"Are you ready?"

Mia looked at Dr. Cortland and nodded. "As I'll ever be."

"You have friends in the room, don't forget that," he said, giving her hand a pat as he moved toward the podium on the riser.

Again she nodded, but there was no sign of Ryan. She tried to banish the disappointment even as the bottom dropped out of her stomach like she'd fallen down an elevator shaft. It didn't matter. In fact, it was better this way. Seeing him in the front row as he'd promised might have made her too nervous to continue. She was going to do this long before she even knew Ryan Mason was here . . . before he'd come back into her life to make her feel every breath like a knife in her lungs again.

Dr. Cortland's voice seemed so far away as he prepared the crowd to accept her presentation. His complimentary statements about her scholarship and her biography made her feel so all alone in the room filled with skeptics and brutal academics, save his colleagues.

When she heard her name called, Mia stood and squared her shoulders, only to turn to see that David had slipped into the back of the room. His eyes held more than their normal disdain. Within them she saw something she didn't want to name. But that also didn't matter. Seeing him there only gave her greater resolve, made her voice firmer, would make her diction crisper, her points said with more confidence. What he'd never understand was that sitting in the back glowering at her wouldn't rattle her; it would only serve to make her dig in and fight for her right to be here.

Yes, she'd given presentations throughout her career with people in the room who felt she didn't have the right to even be in the room and without the benefit of more than one or two friendly faces in the crowd . . . without a spouse or siblings or clapping parents—her people always tethered to an unyielding job. She lifted her chin and cleared her throat as she advanced to the podium, then said a quiet prayer. It was the same prayer she always said: *Por Dios, walk with me.* Then she was strong again.

CHAPTER 12

Thunderous applause led by Dr. Cortland and his colleagues met Mia as she finished and withdrew from the podium. The unnerving thing, however, was that throughout her talk there was a constant stream of unexpected media who'd begun taking photos and seemed to be filming. And each time someone had slipped through the door she'd hoped it was Ryan, but had steeled herself to the fact that he wasn't coming.

Thankfully, Dr. Cortland had established her portion of the program as an information-only session that wouldn't have the normal challenge of Q&A. Her mentor had rightfully concluded that pompous, competitive windbags wanting to appear important or junior academics trying to impress their more senior colleagues wouldn't hesitate to shred her presentation for the sake of their own egos or political maneuvers. A veteran of academic shenanigans, Dr. Cortland had refused to throw her under the bus. More than he could know, this morning she was eternally grateful. But what was all the media about?

"Dr. Austin, Dr. Austin—just one comment about the Times Square bombing attempt," a journalist called out. "Do you think that since the perpetrator failed in his mission this morning, a sleeper cell might make an attempt now that is in line with your theories?"

For a few seconds Mia froze. She'd been so busy going over her presentation this morning that she hadn't turned on the television or the radio in her hotel room. In order to focus she had remained in her room, had coffee and ate fruit, prepping for her talk. Now someone had averted a bombing in Times Square? Oh . . . my . . . God!

Glancing at Dr. Cortland, she did what anyone with a little street savvy and some political instinct would: She winged it.

"I think that this incident clearly demonstrates that the people who have an ax to grind against America will stop at nothing to harm us. My research is just an attempt to make people aware that any vulnerability we have needs to be addressed. Our power grid and our cyber-institutions are at risk. Why wouldn't any weaknesses in our geological infrastructure be a target?"

Her answer set off a barrage of snapshots and a clamor for more.

"Dr. Austin—what about the oil spill in the Gulf—could that have been a terrorist act?"

"Although all accounts by authorities say that it wasn't," Mia replied carefully, "that is the type of thing that could have been. While the spill itself was a horribly tragic accident, something of that catastrophic level—which has far-reaching environmental and economic impact on this country— reveals the scale of damage a natural disaster can wreak. The only difference is that, in the case of the Gulf crisis, eleven lives were unfortunately lost. In a prompted natural disaster, untold numbers of people could be killed or severely injured."

Dr. Cortland moved to her flank as the media crush continued, trying to help escort her to the next session. It took a few frustrating moments to break through the barrier of bodies, but after their flurry the journalists fanned out and cornered the professors whom Dr. Cortland had pointed out as his colleagues. Even though their main focus had been Mia, because he'd described her as the backbone of the research team, they wanted counterpoints and other perspectives.

Mia shook her head as she saw her ex, Dr. David Williams, sucking up his fifteen minutes of fame. It was amazing what a camera and a microphone thrust into someone's face would make them say. No doubt he'd refute everything she'd said and would disparage her in a nice-nasty way in print. Condescending bastard. She couldn't wait to see the blogosphere by tomorrow. Cyberspace was where people could really hack you to death from the anonymity of their laptops rather than confronting you to your face. David was not above such cowardice.

But as she walked beside Dr. Cortland and her mentor fielded questions, Mia's cell phone vibrated loudly in her purse. That's when it hit her: Her mother must be having a conniption!

Quickly digging her cell phone out of her Coach bag, Mia answered it without checking to see who'd called.

"Dr. Austin, this is MSNBC."

Caught off guard, Mia paused. *MSNBC . . . ?*

"Yes . . ."

"Great," an efficient woman on the other end of the phone replied. "I'm Grace Darrow, one of the network's producers, and we were wondering if there was any chance we can get you, with Dr. Cortland, to give us an on-location interview this afternoon down at the Smithsonian in DC, if we send a car for you? Normally we can do it from a video upload studio, or would have had you just come into our studio here at 30 Rockefeller . . . but we'd like to get you in your own environment around the computers and the labs at the Smithsonian, for full effect. Plus, we'll be having a team go over to the Pentagon for location shots there later . . . so your on-location footage would give the piece much more bang. Authenticity, you know?"

"We have a dinner and more workshops to attend at this conference here in New York," Mia said, but then she hesitated as Dr. Cortland caught her attention. "Can you hold a moment, Ms. Darrow?"

"Sure thing," the producer quipped, and immediately Mia heard her typing on her keyboard.

"Mia," Dr. Cortland said in a low murmur into her ear, "which station is it?"

"MSNBC," she replied, holding the phone down low.

"They're national, respected, and the board of directors at the Smithsonian would look very favorably on a young scientist in their employ speaking on a hot subject with one of their emeritus scientists. This is part of the funding game . . . and it will be a very nice career feather for you."

"But they want us to leave the conference to do some on-location stuff in DC *this afternoon.*"

"And?" Dr. Cortland shrugged with a sly smile. "They are sending a car for us, yes?"

"Yes," Mia said, mortified about having to go on television unprepared.

"So we get the transcripts from a few boring lectures and miss a rubber chicken dinner."

Mia chuckled and just shook her head, then brought the cell phone back up to her ear. "Ma'am, I just spoke to my colleague and Dr. Cortland and I would be honored to do the interview."

* * *

Ensconced in the Federal Building around the corner from the Marriott, Ryan stood in the situation room and watched television in horror as Mia's brief comments were embedded in a news frenzy about the Times Square bombing attempt.

Now all the wrong people that were interested in the subject of geological terror knew who she was—and also knew that it was not the crotchety old men with tenure who were the experts. Dr. Cortland had publicly corroborated that his research fellow, Dr. Mia Austin, was the leading scientist on this new area of global threat.

Ryan rubbed both palms down his face. Fatigue and worry for Mia frayed his nerves. He noticed that Ken saw his personal battle from the corner of his eye, and Ken gave Ryan a look that the other agents didn't catch. With a discreet nod, Ryan let Ken know everything would be cool.

But then again, in order for *anything* to be cool they had to get out of these interminable post-suspect-apprehension multiple-agency cluster-fuck meetings and get back to doing what they did best—boots-on-the-ground action. He hated the suits.

"So, this guy we collared," a federal agent said, gaining clarification from his boss, "he's just a wannabe terrorist and has nothing to do with the outfit that masterminded the failed Azores attempt."

"Affirmative," Ryan said, losing patience and answering for the agent's superior. "He might have even been a decoy to get us focused elsewhere while they came for our brain trust." Ryan pushed off the wall where he'd been leaning. "The problem now is that, even with the media information feed delay, faces and names have been clearly identified by interviews broadcast around the world. Along with the other professors, Dr. Austin was just marked as the linchpin in geoterrorism research, and as a result is probably a serious target of interest now."

This time when her cell phone rang, she looked at it. But unlike the last time, she didn't answer. Ryan would have to wait.

Mia climbed into the gleaming black Lincoln Town Car with Dr. Cortland and fastened her seat belt. She couldn't have such a a very personal discussion with her mentor sitting next to her. Besides, it was what it was. Ryan hadn't shown up or called. She had made a complete fool of herself last night . . . had become intimate with Ryan like he was a one-night stand, had gushed all over him emotionally . . . damn. So what was there to say?

That conversation, if there was one to be had at all now, certainly wasn't one that she wanted to get into in front of Dr. Cortland, and talking in code around her mentor would be both obvious and rude. Mia pushed the IGNORE button and put her phone away. Letting the call roll over to voice mail was the best way to handle it.

"I know how you feel," Dr. Cortland said, giving her hand a light pat. "One day you're just doing your research and minding your business and then something unplanned happens to make people take notice. But that's the thing, Mia. People are supposed to take notice of your brilliant mind."

Even though that was the last thing she'd been thinking about, she just smiled and squeezed his supportive, weathered hand.

Ryan expelled an exasperated breath as he crossed the main lobby and headed out of the door. "Come on, pick up," he muttered and then nearly cursed when he got Mia's voice mail.

What else had he expected? If she wasn't pissed off at him for not keeping his promise to be at her presentation, she was no doubt swamped by media or maybe had gone into another session. The hotel was just a few blocks away, and if he could get to her, he'd explain that she needed to lay low and trust him—maybe even leave the conference.

Ken and Ethan had been on his flank, but had peeled off from him to go get their vehicle. For the short distance, his nerves couldn't take the laborious process of getting the thing out of the feds' lot and then creeping around the corner in traffic. Jogging to his destination cleared his mind. He had to get to Mia, and that was all there was to know.

"Mia, it's me—Ryan," he said as soon as he'd pushed the key to bypass her message. "We need to talk. I can't go into it over the phone. But meet me in the lobby."

The moment he hung up, he sent her an abbreviated text with the same message. Now if she'd only hit him back—damn!

Inside the hotel, the lobby was loaded. No sign of Mia. Obviously she hadn't gotten his message or had opted to ignore it. But he spotted two federal agents, and they acknowledged him as he approached.

"You're a bad man," the agent named Joe said, clasping Ryan's hand in a meaty shake.

"You guys did good work out there," Bob said, nodding, and then landed a hand of support on Ryan's shoulder. "Glad we could make it a team effort."

Ryan nodded. "Roger that. But I want you to still keep an eye open on this detail for Dr. Mia Austin. Media just IDed her as the primary researcher on geological terrorism . . . need to make sure she doesn't have crosshairs on her forehead."

The agents gave each other a strange look.

"I thought you took down the bomber and his cronies. There's more of them in the same cell?" Bob said, glancing between Joe and Ryan.

"Yeah," Joe added. "Like, we were told by HQ that for the moment, the threat had been contained."

"I mean, she just walked out of here with the old professor—Dr. Cortland—and got into a Lincoln Town Car not more than twenty minutes ago." Bob shot a nervous glance at Ryan and then looked at his partner for corroboration.

Until now, he'd thought his greatest problem with Mia was going to be how to keep his hands off her. Ryan smoothed his palm over his hair to keep from choking the two agents in front of him. In truth, it wasn't their fault. The communication glitches were rife when trying to dovetail so many agencies on the same mission with everyone having a different chain of command. But if something happened to Mia, he wasn't going to give a rat's ass about process and procedure.

"Listen," he said in a low, firm warning. "The guy we picked up, along with his cronies, was amateur hour. They were acting alone on a glory-seeking mission inspired by some bullshit on the Internet and have no ties to the previous threat we uncovered. That means that every identified civilian at risk is still *at risk*. Copy?"

"Roger that . . . oh, shit," Joe muttered.

Bob pulled out a cell phone and kept his gaze on Ryan. "If we know a general destination, we can get a bird in the air and take you the thoroughfare and mile marker that Lincoln is on, run the tags, and get you through traffic."

"Then you fan out; see if any of the other scientists know where they're headed. I'll do the same. Then we rendezvous by cell to get that chopper in the sky."

CHAPTER 13

For an elderly man, Dr. Cortland appeared to have enough energy to carry the entire conversation by himself. Three and a half hours of nonstop scientific and political banter was giving her a headache behind her left eye. The only call she'd been able to make was to her mother, and the only respite she'd had was while Dr. Cortland was on his cell phone schmoozing with the Smithsonian's president, several members of the board of directors, and her department chair. But even with that she'd had to listen attentively, because all of it was done with a nod and a wink in her direction and on her behalf.

Although she was deeply appreciative, and it was obvious that her mentor loved what he was doing as he so graciously set her up for a meteoric career rise, at the moment she desperately needed some quiet time, just a little space to think and breathe.

Her life had transformed from bland to insanely chaotic in less than twenty-four hours. Her cell phone had been blowing up until she was forced to simply put it on silent, which she had to do because each time it sounded, Dr. Cortland would ask, "Aren't you going to get that?"

The only way to beg her mentor off further questions was to pretend that it was either her girlfriends or family calling about seeing her on TV.

The plan was simple: Ethan would be the lead man from the unit back at the hotel, where there were enough local and federal forces if a problem arose—but there needed to be a Delta Force presence as the tip of the spear. Enough communications missteps had happened to make everybody nervous. Ken would ride shotgun with Ryan down to DC, now that intel had given them a heads-up on Mia and Dr. Cortland's whereabouts. His area of operation would be in DC, but the goal was to take a fallback position and just monitor and protect so as not to tip off Mia and the professor.

The fact that she was riding down to Washington, DC, in a legit car ordered by a known cable news source and on her way to do a live broadcast at her job had let him relax a bit. But the harrowing fifteen minutes it took to learn what he needed to know, depending on both intel and the feds to substantiate that with calls to MSNBC, checking cell phone transmissions, and getting a route and then a visual mark by air on the vehicle in transit, had almost burned an acid hole in his stomach lining.

Then there was the not-so-small fact that Mia was ignoring his calls and text messages. Clearly she was in the Lincoln with only her mentor. Even if she picked up and said she really couldn't talk but would touch base later, he'd know that everything was cool between them. Unfortunately, that wasn't the case.

"You all right, man?" Ken looked at him after breaking rank verbally to speak to him as a friend and not his captain.

Ryan kept his gaze straight ahead on the road as he pressed down on the accelerator. "Affirmative, Lieutenant," he replied, indicating that the unspoken subject was off limits. They were on a mission.

Hours had passed and she felt like the media had picked her brain white-bone clean. It was as though a murder of crows had descended on her mind to tear at the scraps of gray matter that had heretofore been stuffed inside her skull. Even Dr. Cortland looked weary, but dinner with VIPs from the Smithsonian was a must, and the car service left them in the care of their department chair.

"Ian, you look fatigued," Dr. Ross said, calling for the check. "This must have been a completely exhausting but exciting day."

"Aaron, at our age too much excitement can be

both a good and a bad thing. Just like too much wine and rich food can also be a double-edged sword."

Both elderly men chuckled, and Mia stifled a yawn. The rich food at the Mandarin Oriental hotel and fabulous wine and very long day had finally caught up to her.

"My dear," Dr. Cortland said with a smile, "you are far too young to poop out on us after only a couple of glasses of Merlot. But we will revel in your exhaustion, for it makes us old men not feel so ancient."

"I am so sorry," she said, covering her mouth and laughing through a deeper yawn. "I was up at dawn prepping for my talk and the night before it, I didn't rest that well. It isn't the wonderful company, it's nervous energy finally having run its course."

"My goodness," Dr. Ross said, placing his linen napkin beside his plate. "Surely you cannot claim presentation jitters or stage fright as a reason for staying up all night."

Mia froze but smiled, guilt clawing at her and unsure of where Dr. Ross was headed. He gave her an amiable guffaw and took a sip of wine.

"You, Dr. Austin, are a natural. You handled the media like a pro . . . my wife has been instructed to TiVo every show that your interview will air on. All I'm hearing are good things all around, and I'm told that you had them eating out of the palm of your hand in New York."

"Thank you, sir," Mia replied in a quiet tone.

"But I'm sure that was an exaggeration by some of my colleagues who are very enthusiastic about my research." She gave Dr. Cortland a warm smile and watched him fold his hands over his round belly like a satisfied elf.

"No," Dr. Ross continued. "I was a witness of your interview segment and saw how absolutely articulate you were. I must say, I was surprised and impressed."

From the corner of her eye she saw Dr. Cortland's expression cloud over. She knew it rankled him no end when people inadvertently used certain phrases and spoke of how articulate she was, as though she were supposed to be illiterate or use a combination of Spanglish and Ebonics. But she was feeling too good and was way too tired to get into any of that with her blue-blooded department chair. Hell, before today, the man had thought her research was near crackpot and only suffered it or her because Dr. Cortland had been a staunch advocate. So rather than say anything politically incorrect, she just smiled.

"Thank you, Dr. Ross. Your support of my work means everything."

"You are more than welcome," Dr. Ross replied, completely oblivious to any verbal slight. "We see big things in the future for you here, Mia."

"Yes, well, this tired soul sees an immediate future in a little rest after a long day," Dr. Cortland said in a slightly churlish tone.

"Of course, Ian." Dr. Ross hailed the waiter with a flourish of his wrist. "Would you like me to see you home or would you simply prefer to stay here for the evening to make your return commute to the conference easier? On the department, of course."

"We'll take that as an offer we cannot refuse," Dr. Cortland said, his mood slightly improving.

"Thank you for everything," Mia chimed in, "although I do reserve the right to jump in a cab and run home for a moment to gather a few items in an overnight bag."

"Ah, the fairer sex," Dr. Cortland said with a droll smile. "Us gray-hairs need only a few hotel-provided toiletries and we have no problem recycling the prior day's wear. Yet I am not offended that this would be appalling to you, and I would expect nothing less from a lady." He lifted Mia's hand to his lips and bowed where he sat to kiss the back of it. "To your chariot, milady . . . a yellow cab after you check in. A wise choice indeed. Whereas I will use that same time to burp and release other gases in privacy and then go directly to sleep."

The threesome laughed as Dr. Ross paid the bill. There were so many times that Dr. Cortland reminded her of an academically cultured version of her late father that she just wanted to hug him.

"Captain, we've got a problem," Ken said, glancing at Ryan as he lowered his night-vision goggles.

"Only the department chair came out and handed the valet a ticket. Dr. Austin is on the move—the hotel staffer is hailing her a cab."

"Which means Cortland is staying the night." Ryan looked at Ken and started the motor. "We need to split up."

Ken popped the lock on his door. "You don't even have to say it, Cap. I'll stay here with Cortland, will get intel on his room number, and will monitor him here while you shadow Dr. Austin."

Mia paid the cabbie and quickly shut the car door behind her. Just her luck tonight to get a very nice but very talkative old man when all she wanted to do was veg out and stare at the cityscape as it passed her by. As she mounted the steps to her now beloved apartment, home had never looked so good. She wondered why her life always seemed to be a series of extremes. But none of that mattered as she opened the front door and the most consistent love of her life leaped into her arms.

"I missed you, too, you bad boy," Mia crooned, although a little startled by Max's unexpected affection. "What are you doing down here? I bet you gave Camille the ol' slip, huh?"

Oddly, Max still seemed jumpy in her hold, strangely agitated as though he wanted her but also wanted to now get down. She held him firmly and marched up the stairs to her apartment, noticing that the light on the top landing was out. Just fine.

Good thing she'd come home, because Camille wouldn't know how to navigate her keys in the dark like she'd occasionally had to. But normally her downstairs neighbors who were home all day were on it.

"What's wrong with you, boy? I was only gone one . . ."

Mia's words trailed off as she spotted her apartment door hanging ajar off its hinges. She spun, holding Max tighter, the goal to run back down the stairs and into the street. But a force like a brick wall stopped her. A hand clamped over her mouth. Max hissed and fled her arms. For a few seconds she panic-twisted to get free and then began to jab her elbows to find any soft area on the body behind her that she could slam.

"Don't move and don't scream," a deep male voice whispered into her ear. He gripped her harder as her thrashes became wilder.

The voice was remotely familiar, but pure terror blocked any formal recognition.

"Mia, it's me. Ryan."

That didn't make her panic reside, only escalated it to an entirely new level of fear. He'd stalked her? An ex-vet who knew how to kill people with his bare hands . . . one with self-professed career issues. *Jesus Christ.* She'd heard about guys like this who'd done one too many tours of duty only to come home and go around the bend. Now this crazy SOB had his hand over her mouth, had broken into her apartment, and was about to attack her in a darkened hallway. Mother Mary of God hear her prayer. What if he didn't retire from the military, but was put out on a psychiatric? After ten years she didn't know jack shit about this man!

Mia stopped struggling, hoping that if she seemed like she was yielding he would release his hold on her. Maybe she could talk him down the steps, talk herself out the front door. Something. Anything. Or if he dragged her into her apartment, maybe there she could get to a kitchen knife or a lamp. Her mind whirred options as her chest heaved up and down.

"I'm not going to hurt you," he whispered. "But you have to stay quiet for your own safety. All right?"

That's what all serial killers said. They all claimed they'd let you go and wouldn't hurt you if you just acted like a good girl. Still Mia found herself nodding—hope colliding with terror—as tears streamed down her cheeks and she felt Ryan's grip loosen.

The second he let her go, he whipped out the biggest gun she'd ever seen. The scream she'd had pent up now caught in her throat. She covered her own mouth with both hands and simply shook her head. The only thing that escaped her was a gasp and the muffled word, "Please . . ."

Oddly, he stepped around her and put a finger to his lips, then pressed his body to the wall, advancing toward the door with his weapon pointed away from her. He motioned for her to get down and somewhere in the fragile moments of watching him slide toward her ajar apartment door, getting farther away from her as he directed her with hand signals to get down, slow clarity began to penetrate her traumatized mind.

Instead of fleeing, she moved to the far dark corner where Max was crouched hissing, spitting mad, and lowered her body to the floor. She heard things banging, like Ryan was kicking in doors commando-style. Mia covered her head, minutes ticking away like hours. Panic sweat drenched her body; her cat was wild-eyed and unapproachable. Then it was over. Ryan reappeared in the hallway and said two words that made her feel faint.

"All clear."

She slowly uncovered her head and looked up at him. Her eyes must have said it all, because he came to her, but she drew back, scrambling to her feet, reacting very much like Max.

"Back off and explain," she said, pressing her body to the adjacent wall, her eyes never leaving the huge pistol he was clutching.

"I'll explain inside. We need to get you out of here."

"Oh, hell fucking no," she said, edging toward the stairs.

He body-blocked her and kept his voice low.

"You're in serious danger and it's my job to protect you. That's all I can tell you out here in the hall."

Mia stared at the gun. "So, what is it . . . you got busted in the service for moving heroin or coke from Turkey or Afghanistan or some crazy shit like that, and now whoever you owe is looking for where you might have stashed it? You tell 'em I was your woman or something, so they wouldn't raid your mom's place?" She could feel her voice escalating, could feel the veins standing up in her neck.

Before she could bolt or scream, he'd stashed the weapon and was on her so quickly that she turned her face and covered it with her arms, expecting a blow.

"No, Mia," he said in a low, sharp stab of breath into her ear. "I would never betray you, myself, my family, my people, or my country like that. Now let's move."

She slowly took her arms down, still unsure. "You said you had career issues . . ."

He took her by the hand, leaned in close, and whispered his response. "Your research has put you in danger. I lied. Okay. I never retired from the military. I'm Delta Force and you're my asset of value to protect. We will not be calling the police. This has to go directly to the feds, so they can sweep this apartment. Military intelligence will—"

"Military intelligence . . . ," she said in a harsh whisper, snapping her head up to stare at him.

He took out his weapon and placed it in her hands. "Military issue. If I was going to attack you or shoot you, would I hand this to you, Mia?"

The metal he'd placed in her hands was so heavy she'd almost dropped it. For a moment, she just stared at him.

"Can I get an overnight change of clothes and get my cat?"

He carefully took his gun back from her and nodded, leading the way back into her apartment. "Try not to touch anything except the edges of the drawers. The closet is already open."

Mia stood in her living room, mouth agape. Her sofa was overturned, the cushions slashed. Artwork was slashed, every cabinet in her kitchen was open, and all the drawers were pulled out and dumped. Her refrigerator and freezer sat open. She couldn't move.

"You didn't do this, did you?" she asked slowly as realization dawned.

"No, it was clearly someone looking for something they didn't find here," Ryan muttered. "Good thing no one was here."

"Camille," Mia said in a rush and then frantically dug in her bag.

Ryan crossed the room as soon as she got out her cell phone and held her hand.

"You call your girlfriend and tell her that you came home to find your apartment robbed . . . and that you'll bring your cat to her—but she is not under any circumstances to come back here. Then you tell her you have to go make a police report. Do not stay on the phone. Assure her you're all right, then tell her not to worry anyone else in your family. Got it?"

Mia nodded and made the call, listening to Camille's shrieks of disbelief as she tried to quickly convey the information. Ryan typed a text message into his phone and didn't push SEND, but simply showed the question to Mia to convey to Camille.

"Uh, Camille," Mia said, still shaken. "What time did you get here to feed and water Max?"

"Like six thirty," she responded.

"Oh, right after work, then?" Mia kept her eyes on Ryan. "Like always."

"Yeah," Camille said, her voice tight with worry. "So if anybody busted in there, it had to be way after that."

"All right, thanks," Mia said, her eyes still fastened to Ryan's. "But don't upset my mom and whatnot. And more than anything, don't come back here. It's obviously not safe. I'll bring Max to you."

"Okay," Camille replied in a soft voice. "You be careful. I am so sorry all this happened to you. I'll be waiting up."

Mia stood in the middle of the room for a moment just holding her cell phone and staring at Ryan, in shock.

"What do you need to pack?" he said, going to

her and leading her by the hand toward her bedroom. "Mia, we've gotta keep it moving."

She followed his lead but stopped again as she saw the wreckage that lay before her. Everything was sliced and turned over.

"I feel so violated," she whispered, not knowing where to begin.

Ryan walked over to what was left of her dresser. "Jeans to travel in?" he asked, not addressing her comment. "Underwear. A shirt." He looked at her feet. "Running shoes, socks, and a gym bag. The hotel will give you a toothbrush, toothpaste, and deodorant."

She simply watched him as he grabbed the items he'd mentioned while she stood transfixed at the door. But when he picked up her underwear, she turned her head.

"I'll never put that next to my body. They stepped on it and God knows what else."

"Wash out the ones you're wearing and blow-dry them with the hotel's appliance."

Fury at the invasion flooded her system, and with nowhere else for it to go, she lashed out at him. "Sounds like you've done this before."

Ryan took the charge stoically. "Unfortunately, baby, I have." He thrust her bag in her direction and she accepted it, although it didn't contain the jeans she would have chosen, the shirt she would have chosen, the socks she would have chosen, or the sneakers she'd wanted to wear. "Get the cat."

"Easier said than done," she said in a sullen tone and walked through her apartment.

"Do you want me to get him?" Ryan said, giving her a sidelong glance.

"No. Like me, he's already been traumatized enough."

CHAPTER 14

Mia sat as still as stone riding beside Ryan with Max on her lap cowering in his carrying cage. She so hated to do that to the little guy, but it was the best thing for everyone involved. Max had strongly objected to going anywhere as long as the huge dude with the gun was with her, which only made Mia wonder what the guys who'd kicked down her door looked like.

Coded military speak made her strain to understand what Ryan was saying about her, about Dr. Cortland—about the whole situation, in fact. However, she kept before her the goal that, once she'd told Camille good-bye and handed off Max, she'd ask Ryan a million questions for sure.

"If she asks, I'm a cop," Ryan said as Mia got out by the curb.

Mia never answered. Camille was already at the

door, standing on the landing in a robe. She'd promised herself she wouldn't cry as she bounded up the steps, set Max's cage down, and hugged Camille hard.

"Come in here—damn whoever says what, you're staying here with me!"

"I can't," Mia said, holding her girlfriend tightly. "I have to go back to the uhmmm . . . precinct to do the report and then they've gotta sweep my place. Just watch my baby for me, and I *promise* to call you tomorrow once I get some shuteye."

"Where are you going to get some shuteye?" Camille said, horrified as she held Mia away from her.

"I'm gonna go back to the conference. I have to. I can't let the fact that someone broke into my apartment totally throw away a career opportunity like this. I'll sleep on the train and miss the morning sessions. All right?"

Camille kissed her cheek. "I guess . . ." She smoothed back Mia's hair. "You did look really fly on the news and, girl, you tore it up on MSNBC."

Both women found a way to laugh. Leave it to crazy Camille to make even the worst of circumstances seem all right.

"That's probably how they knew to break into my house. I was on the news, *duh*."

"Oh, yeah! Damn . . . I didn't even think about that." Camille shook her head. "You have insurance, right?"

"Girl, you know me." Mia tried to look upbeat.

Camille didn't know the half of it. They stole nothing but had destroyed everything. She had no idea what they'd been looking for, but they'd taken her sense of security in the process. She doubted she'd ever feel safe in her own home again.

"That's bullshit that you get your fifteen minutes of fame and some jerk steals your big screen and DVR so you can't even watch the damned broadcast of yourself." Camille placed a hand on her hip and struck a sassy pose. "Some people just get on my last nerve!"

"Okaaaay." Mia hugged Camille again. "I've gotta go. The detective in the black car has an attitude." She picked up Max and made kissy faces at him. "Be easy with my boy . . . he may flee the cage and just stay under your bed till I get back."

"No worries. Me and ol' Max are cool. I'll tempt him out with salmon tomorrow, but will leave a fresh litterbox in the corner of whatever room he decides to make his lair."

"Thanks . . . I don't know how to—"

"Don't say another word and get all mushy on me. I'm not trying to cry anymore tonight, girl. Now go on. Maybe you'll meet some tall, fine, chocolate hunk in the precinct."

Mia pushed Camille away, laughing, as her friend leaned past her to squint at the waiting vehicle. "Go in the house!"

"I'm just saying . . ." Camille picked up Max and stuck her tongue at him. "Hey, you've always had a weakness for guys in uniform. Who knows, maybe all this happened for a reason?"

"Good night, Miss Camille," Mia said with a smile, and then turned and ran down the steps.

Her smile instantly faded the moment her back was to Camille. Ryan had been right, though—the less innocent civilians knew about any of this craziness in her life, the safer they'd be. She turned once as she reached the black vehicle, forced a smile, and waved to her friend. Then without a word she climbed into the seat and shut the door, thankful for tinted windows.

"I'll need your mother's current address, her place of employ, same with your siblings, and I'll need to know where your girlfriend works."

Mia just stared at him for a second as he drove.

"If someone wants you badly enough, and for some reason can't get to you, one surefire way to smoke you out of hiding is to have a loved one place a panic call . . . or make you have to visit a hospital or attend a funeral."

Mia stopped breathing.

"So I need to call in that information so local law enforcement can help keep an eye on your VIP list."

Words still failed her.

"I'm not trying to scare you—but I need to be sure you understand how important it is for you to help me keep you safe until we find these bastards."

"How long have I been under surveillance?"

The magnitude of it all, the invasion of her privacy, the loss of her freedom: All of it suddenly brought clarity to her mind and sharpness to her tongue. "When, Ryan!"

He looked at her briefly before turning back to navigate through traffic. "The last person I expected to see again in that hotel was you . . . and the last person I thought I'd have on my potential hostage list was you. Cortland was my high-value asset. Then you walked into the lobby and jacked my focus up. Everything changed. The mission changed."

She hugged herself and stared out the front window. "So, like when they said a Vietnam vet saw the smoking car in Times Square, he wasn't a vendor." It wasn't a question, but delivered as more of a statement as her mind dissected the fragments of information she did have. "He was one of your military spooks."

When Ryan didn't respond, she gave him a sidelong glance.

"And I bet you guys probably caught the guy at least twenty-four hours before you leaked a bogus story about how it all went down to the press." Mia stopped hugging herself and folded her arms over her chest, getting angrier by the moment. "What? If you tell me you'd have to kill me?"

"Something like that," Ryan replied in a flat, sarcastic tone.

"So, everything that happened yesterday was

just one big lie all worked out in some war room somewhere, huh."

"Not everything," he muttered and then pressed down extra hard on the brakes when they came to a red light, jerking the vehicle to a halt.

"Really? You mean there was no pushpin of Mia on some jumbo strategic whiteboard that said: Mason—keep the subject occupied by whatever means nec—"

"No!"

His voice was like a subsonic boom that she felt in the pit of her stomach. Without warning he pulled the vehicle out of traffic and into an open spot by the curb.

"Two things," he said, gripping the steering wheel tightly. "I never lied to you about how I felt about you—ever. And number two, I wouldn't let my command know about any of that. I could probably be court-marshaled for what happened in your room. You are a civilian and I am the property of the U.S. government."

Mia looked away from his intense gaze. "So, you're not a professor at NYU, you don't work with kids . . . never did."

"No, Mia," he said plainly. "I wish I did have that option, but right now I don't. Who wouldn't love a job like that, but what I do for a living makes sure there will be colleges and universities and everything else we hold dear over here. We're in the middle of a war. Your brilliant research helped to shed light on an area where we're vulnerable. But as a result, it's also made you vulnerable. Understand?"

"But why couldn't you just tell me when we were alone?" Her gaze searched his until he looked away.

"The mission was classified." Ryan closed his eyes and leaned his head back against the seat. "We were supposed to take a fallback position. I tried to frame it by saying I had 'career issues,' and believe me, right now, I do. I thought I could give you intel on a need-to-know basis, and then once this was done, I'd have time to explain. But *nothing* about this has gone according to plan. The last thing I expected was to look up and see you on cable. *Jesus*."

Ryan rubbed his palms down his face and sat forward. "I tried to call you, but you wouldn't answer my calls."

"I thought after last night, you'd decided things were too intense, I was too needy or something and—"

"Mia, look at me," he said, opening his arms. His tone was firm but his voice and eyes were gentle. "Do you remember what I had on yesterday?"

She allowed her gaze to rove over his clothing. "That's what you had on before."

"Correct," he said, turning away to rest his forehead on the steering wheel. "That is what I had on yesterday, because all night I've been climbing through alleys, kicking in fucking doors, and dragging one sorry sonofabitch to justice. That's why I couldn't keep my promise. I was on the job, so to speak. So whatever reason you've concocted about why I wasn't there for the presentation was wrong."

He turned his head and looked at her. Now it was her turn to send her gaze out of the tinted windows.

"I thought—"

"That Ryan Mason was some no-good, low-life brother with a long story and thin ego who couldn't stand to see a woman get her professional due, right?"

When she didn't answer, he shifted the gears into reverse and backed up, then hard-wrenched the vehicle into drive.

"I'm not like that sorry bastard that I dropped in the street on your behalf last night. Don't get it twisted."

"I know that," she said quietly.

"Really?" He jerked the car to a stop again, half in and half out of the parking space. "Oh, no, that's right. David is the intellectual—I'm thug brother, the one who's got the proclivity to run contraband from Turkey or Afghanistan or wherever the hell I've been for ten years, right? The dude from Bed-Stuy. The guy who has to be ready to rob you in the darkened hallway of your apartment building—or rape you—the guy who has his drug thug friends ready to take revenge by shooting you, right?"

He turned away with outrage glittering in his eyes and then pulled the vehicle into traffic.

"I didn't—"

"Just drop that part, Mia. It was written all over your face. I never want to see you look at me like that again in my life."

"I'm sorry, but . . . what was I supposed to think?" Her voice was becoming shaky as she watched the anger in his expression morph into a level of hurt she knew all too well. The pain of being stereotyped by circumstances and accident of birth.

"How about trusting in me?" he finally said in a quiet tone. "I'd asked that one thing of you last night and you said you'd do that."

"Not fair," she shot back, but her tone had lost all of its sharp condemnation. She turned and looked at him, even though he wasn't looking at her. "I had just come out of something really bad where the person I was with had plenty of ego issues with seeing me achieve anything on my own. Then someone comes back into my life, we have a very intense intimate encounter, then from what I can tell, he disappears—only to reappear by blowing up my phone. Then someone who I think should be in New York is at *my apartment*?"

Mia sat back, her tone conciliatory but holding no apology in it. "This same guy who's built like he's in the Green Berets or whatever—now I know it's Delta Force—same diff to me . . . has a gun, my hall light is blown out. He's holding my face so I can't scream. I can see my apartment has been broken into. Oh, yeah, and did I mention, home-boy has already told me he has career issues. And I'm from the city . . . where does my mind go? Be honest."

Ryan gave her a curt nod.

"My female brain processes danger like this, Ryan. Psycho. Weapon. Body like a brick wall. On a rampage when I didn't answer his calls and texts. Anger out of control. What have I gotten myself into? Please, Jesus, don't let him hit me. I'll need a wire for my jaw. My face will be crushed. Look at the size of his hands. He can beat me to death with those hands. More than that, whatever he does, let it be quick. Ex-military, clearly unstable. Trained killer. Forget trying to grab a knife or a lamp, that'll just piss him off. Yield your body and beg. Give him whatever he wants; tell him whatever he wants to hear. Live to see another day. Only chance is to get the weapon. You probably can't outrun him. Gotta put the bastard down with a bullet."

She hugged herself again and stared out the window. "If I had your strength and your skill and a weapon in my hand, maybe I wouldn't have been as afraid. But don't you get all high and mighty because I almost peed my pants. I had every right to be afraid."

"I'm sorry," he said quietly. "Is that what you really thought?"

She spun on him, tears suddenly filling her eyes. "Yes! Look at you and look at me! In hand-to-hand combat, I'm no match for you!"

"Mia, I've never ever laid a hand on a woman like that. Seen it done to my mom. I can't even go there. But pity the bastard that ever puts his hands on her again."

Mia swallowed hard and lifted her chin. "I got so-called bitch-slapped in my face, once. That was when I really understood the strength difference between a man and a woman."

"Who?" Ryan stopped at a light and only the honking of cars behind him made him realize that he needed to move again.

"It doesn't matter. You already got one in for me."

"David?"

"The breakup was ugly, like I said. He called me a bunch of names, and I went straight Harlem and said, 'Yo, momma.' Next thing I knew I was tasting blood. End of story."

"I don't care what you said to him, he had no right to put his hands on you."

"Yeah, well, I'm not Cinderella. A lot of things that go down in the fairy tales don't happen in real life."

"I can show you self-defense moves that aren't size-dependent. I can also show you how to kill a mofo with a pencil—which, given the circumstances, wouldn't be a bad skill to have . . . just promise not to flip out and use it on me. Deal?"

She gave him another sidelong glance, noticing a slight smile playing around the corners of his mouth. It drew a small one out on her face, yet she was anything but okay.

"All right, I'll take you up on that training," she said, her smile fading as she spoke. "But who the hell is after me? What did I do that makes me a target?"

Ryan's expression became serious and he took up her hand with one of his, driving with his left. "There are some really bad guys out there who want the details on the research you've done, specific co-ordinates and information about how to set off a catastrophic geological event under one of our major cities here in the U.S. These guys will do anything to get it. We took some of them down, but not all of them. But rest assured, now that I know they're after you . . . it's gone way beyond my job, it's personal."

CHAPTER 15

Paranoia made every muscle in Mia's body tense as she crossed the lobby of the Mandarin Oriental hotel and spoke to the desk clerk. Knowing that Ryan was hanging back but nearby made her feel better. But knowing that she could be abducted totally freaked her out.

Still, the soothing tone of the ebullient staffer helped calm her. The young woman didn't raise an eyebrow when Mia walked in, slightly disheveled, one small bag over her shoulder, and a very tall, very fine, stone-hewn man obviously with her— one who looked like he'd exerted himself in some physical activity . . . and now she was asking for double toothpaste and other complimentary toiletries. She must've looked very calm checking in earlier after dinner with a significantly older gentleman, and now she was checking in under a totally different name with cash—courtesy of Ryan's military contacts.

However, this was indeed Washington, DC, where discretion was the better part of valor and the staff members of the best hotels kept poker expressions and had seemingly blind eyes. Tonight she was thankful for that as Ryan followed her to the elevator. She just prayed that Dr. Cortland had gone to bed and that their rooms were on vastly different floors.

Silence surrounded her and Ryan as they stood side by side and then exited the elevator to locate her room. This was so different from the butterflies that had been in her belly the night before. Right now all sexual tension had been replaced by trauma nausea.

When she went to open the door, he held his hand out for the key. "Just as a precaution."

Mia nodded and gave it to him. She was way beyond arguing with the man. The only thing she had enough energy for was some herbal tea to settle her stomach, and maybe a good shower; then her plan was to collapse.

Waiting until Ryan cased the room and gave her the silent all-clear with a quick motion of his chin, Mia slipped past the door behind him and sighed. Ryan had booked a spacious, premier water-view room that was nestled into one of the building's corners. A palate of soft gold tones met her, and the floor-to-ceiling windows that overlooked the marina simply made her drop her gym bag to the floor in awe. A beautiful, salmon-hued chaise longue bookended by the windows faced a sumptuous king-size bed adorned with satin Asian-themed pillows.

"Wow . . . ," she murmured, standing in the room in the dark.

"Windows are a bit of a problem," he said, "but if we keep the main lights off and no one knows you're here, you should be all right. At least this high up with a view of the Potomac, there's no building platform for a sniper."

"They want to kill me now?"

"No. Just anyone with you. You're good—just can't let them abduct you."

She couldn't even respond. Mia hoisted her small bag to a chair and then went to check out the bathroom. Opulent pale gray Chinese marble stared back at her as she flipped on the light. A huge soaking tub took up one corner, and a separate all-glass stall shower with both wall-mounted and handheld showerheads greeted her. The tub had her name written all over it.

"Listen," she said, coming out of the bathroom to face Ryan. "I'm tired, you're tired, but I refuse to be so terrorized that my entire life is just taken over by these unseen people. I want to make a cup of tea, unwind my wrecked nerves, and sit in the tub. All right?"

"No problem . . . but why are you saying that to me as though I'm the enemy?"

A half smile tugged at his cheek, and it made her take her hands off her hips and simply hug herself.

"Because I'm tired and evil and really pissed off that these people, who have no right, can just change a person's life because *they* are crazy!" Releasing her hold on herself, she began talking with her hands. "I was minding my business, doing what I love—research. What right do they have to come over here with their bullshit?"

"None whatsoever," he said with a calm shrug. "This is why me and my unit do what we do. My motto is the same as it was when I was a kid growing up in Brooklyn—*Don't start none, won't be none.*"

"Right," she said, feeling better that he agreed.

"You said you wanted some tea."

"Yeah, I do," she said in a calmer voice, "but you know what, I bet you're exhausted."

"If I admit to it, I might pass out," he said, rubbing his palm over his hair. "But, hey, sleeping on deep-pile carpet in the Mandarin sure beats some of the places I've had to bed down."

She stared at him, really taking in his words. "Thank you," she said in a quiet tone. "Not just for what you did for me, but what you do for all of us."

"It goes with the territory," he said with a self-conscious shrug.

"No. It doesn't. You could have decided to do anything with a fabulous education coming out of

West Point. You could have done your time in uniform and then transitioned into a thousand different jobs . . . but you chose to continue to protect and serve . . . and I owe you an apology for freaking out so hard."

"No apologies. Remember? Besides, until you broke it down for me just what runs through a woman's head when cornered by what seems like a dangerous male, I didn't really get it. I would have been freaked out, too, if the roles were reversed. Mia, I am so sorry that I had to do that to you—and even sorrier that this is even happening to you at all."

"You have no control over the state of the world and the crazies in it, Ryan . . . even though, if one of those rat bastards comes after me, I do hope you're Superman. Like, I won't be mad if you leap tall buildings with a single bound or devise some MacGyver-type escape—just sayin'."

He laughed, which made her laugh, and for the first time since everything had gone down she felt like there was still some semblance of normalcy in her life.

"Look, why don't you go get a shower, use one of these fancy robes they've got in the closet, and I'll make you a cup of Joe . . . I can even order you some room service, if you're hungry."

"Oh . . . maaan," he murmured, closing his eyes. "Don't tempt me, Mia. But I can't have you open the door while I'm in the shower. That's the perfect time for somebody to come in here."

"It'll take half an hour and if they come before that, I'll just open the door with that huge gun."

Now he laughed in earnest. "I could use a cup of coffee and a burger. Leave my gun on the table and just give me fifteen minutes, all right?"

"Deal," she said, glad that there was something she could do to let the man know she did appreciate all he'd done, even if it had taken her a while to show it.

"But I thought you wanted to take a bath?" His question brought him to a skidding halt.

"I do, and you know how long women take in the bathroom, so I'm being chivalrous and letting you go first." She winked at him and went to find the coffeemaker. "I'll hook up your Joe, and by the time you're out, you can have a hot cup. Then I'll dump what you don't drink and make my tea and settle down for a very long date with some bubbles. Meanwhile, you can receive your burger via room service and can scare the poor waiter if you want, and eat and watch TV or whatever. Fair?"

"I wish you were my logistics commander," he said with a bright smile. "That's more than fair."

Mia watched him slip into the bathroom and shut the door and then kicked out of her shoes. She went to the window in the dark, looking out at the diamonds of lights that twinkled in the distance. Washington was so beautiful, yet beneath the veneer of calm and control was so much insanity. A history of wars, political double-dealing and duplicity, summits and conferences and treaties and the Secret Service—all of it was just as much a part of the landscape as was the White House. And yet, no matter what, every year the cherry blossoms bloomed anyway. People raised their children. Folks visited the spectacular monuments. Tour buses jammed the streets . . . and life went on.

She listened to the shower go on and after a moment went to find the coffeemaker. Maybe that was the whole point. Life went on, no matter what. And some people, people like Ryan who'd committed their lives to ensure that happened, were an important but often unseen part of the whole tapestry.

After a second, she realized that although the room was huge, it wasn't a suite. It didn't have a secondary water source. She'd have to wait until he came out to make his coffee. She didn't dare trust her mind to walk in on him. Mia shook her head and laughed to herself. With her luck, she might get shot. Then again, she could knock . . .

Rather than create more drama, she phoned in his room service order, needing something constructive to do with the sudden surge of energy that hit her. By the time she hung up the room phone, the shower had stopped. She grabbed the coffeepot and crossed the room to sit on the chaise longue. He was out in a heartbeat. Obviously the military taught him to do perfunctory man-time activities at super-speed.

But rather than get up quickly to go get the

water, she just sat quietly for a moment with the glass coffeepot held midair, slack-jawed.

The bathroom light backlit him, making his semi-sweet dark chocolate skin glisten from the droplets of water that ran down his shoulders and chest. A thick, stark white terry towel was slung low around his waist, showing off every brick in his abdomen, all the way down to the well-defined oblique cord of muscle that ran from his lower abdominals right into his groin. Have mercy . . . he'd come out of the celestial light half naked with a gun in one hand, beads of water raining from his hair and sluicing down a pair of shoulders that could have easily been carved out of the bathroom marble.

A sheepish grin offered her a glimpse of that trademark white smile of his. Try as she might, she couldn't help but to allow her gaze free rein to travel down the length of his body, over the relaxed but impressive bulge in his towel, down massive, corded thighs and well-proportioned calves. Now she could clearly see why some people got more done by five A.M. than every frickin' body else in the world.

"I'll get the bathroom back in shape—but I was in such a rush to hit the water that I forgot to grab a robe out of the closet. Sorry. Just give me a minute."

"Take your time," she said in a near rasp. *Daaaaayum.*

She watched him turn around and go to the closet, mesmerized by the network of muscles that made his arms move. It was as though his shoulder blades were giant, steel cable pulleys that lifted iron biceps. His back was pure artwork, down to the valley that created a ridge on either side of his spine down to the dip that gave rise to an outrageously magnificent ass.

Her mouth had gone dry by the time she turned around, and then he pulled a move that made the coffeepot tremble in her grasp. He simply donned the robe, whipped off the towel, tied the sash, and stuffed his pistol in the pocket.

"Will get all the water off the floor and toothpaste out of the sink," he said, gesturing with the towel he'd obviously intended to use for the job. "By the time you come out, I'll have on my duds again."

It took her a moment to answer but she found her voice protesting. Put clothes on? Why . . . ?

"But you just took a shower and those clothes are filthy," she said, laughing. "At least wouldn't you want to get a good night's sleep more comfortably?"

"Yeah, but if something goes down or I get a call, I've gotta be ready to roll."

"At least eat first," she said, trying to sound casual as she followed him into the bathroom and went to the sink.

For a moment she just watched him do a squat in the robe to grab his clothes. As he stood, he kicked down the toilet seat.

"Sorry about that. Normally don't have to worry about it."

She turned back to the coffeepot, which was now almost full, and hurriedly shut off the water. "Hey, that's the least of our concerns, right? I'll get that coffee going and your burger should be here shortly."

"Cool."

Flustered, she gave herself some distance by getting out of the too-close confines to fiddle with the coffeemaker. But she noticed him sitting in a chair way across the room and trying to get comfortable in it while flipping on the TV.

"I think for punching out my ex, who was being a jerk, taking me to dinner, buying some great hotel munchies at the supermarket, then what . . . taking a Black Hawk helicopter or something to DC top find me and save my life—in case al-Qaeda was looking for me—warrants that you can stretch out and watch a football game or whatever sports season it is. Just saying." She smiled at him and got the coffee brewing and was rewarded by his warm chuckle.

He rubbed his jaw and then shook his head. "You've got me breaking all kinds of rules."

She gave him a shrug for an answer. "Just trying to show some appreciation."

A knock at the door put him on his feet, and she watched how he went to answer it. He stood on the side of the door, not directly in front of it, and waited until the server announced that it was room service. Glancing out the peephole quickly, he relaxed and opened the door. Again, one of the hallmarks of the better hotels in the area was that staff kept a poker face, no matter how strange the guests seemed. Mia paid the bill with the cash he'd given her and added a tip; the server simply thanked her and backed out of the door.

"You added a cola to the order," Ryan said in awe, staring down at the silver-domed food.

"I figured you'd want it with the burger and the game . . . then if you still wanted coffee, okay. Double caffeine, since you're trying to stay awake."

"Did I mention you're an angel and the best asset of value I've ever been assigned to protect."

"I could answer that in a number of ways, but I will decline comment."

They both laughed as he brought the rolling tray to the foot of the bed and popped the tab on the Coke. A remote in one hand, he pointed it at the large HDTV flatscreen and sat down, and then pulled the cover off the burger and inhaled.

"Maaaan, I am so far off base and so far off duty . . ."

"Knock yourself out," she said, going to the closet to get a robe. "I'll be in there until my skin wrinkles up."

"You're not hungry?" he asked with a mouthful of fries.

"No, just some tea is cool."

"Aw, man. Right." He stood and walked over to the coffeepot. "I'll dump it. I'm good with the cola."

"You might want it after you eat. You haven't slept in twenty-four hours or more, so . . . maybe on a commercial break, after you eat. You could bring it to me. I'll be under the bubbles."

He gave her a sidelong glance and took a sip from his Coca-Cola Can. "Dangerous, but possible."

"As tired as we both are, and given all we've been through," she said laughing, "I don't think it's all that dangerous."

He nodded, his wide smile capturing the can's opening. "Yeah, okay, if you say so, Dr. Austin."

CHAPTER 16

Once inside the spacious bathroom, Mia shed her clothes and ran the bathwater. A tempting array of bath toiletries greeted her. She opened the cap on the shower gel and nearly moaned as she inhaled the rich fragrance. The scent of it was divine, enough to leave her heady. After the day she'd had, the Mandarin lavishly offered Gilchrist & Soames soaps, lotions, shampoo, and conditioner. A little bit of luxury was definitely the American way of life, and no terrorist was going to rob her of this bit of heaven.

Neatly folding her dirty clothes in a pile next to the sink, she took great care to hand-launder her bra and panties and hang them neatly on the edge of the glass shower stall. She could definitely get used to this: a life with a little luxury and really genuine male companionship—albeit sans insane terrorists.

Banishing the less appealing aspects of her thoughts, she climbed into the warm tub that was by now overflowing with bubbles, sank down neck-deep, closed her eyes, and groaned. The heat from the water and the blissful fragrance all around her was nearly enough to melt her bones. With great effort she turned off the spigot and resettled herself. Only now did she realize how much tension she'd been carrying in every muscle fiber. Places hurt that shouldn't have as the contracted areas of her body slowly began to ease out their knots.

Tight walnuts of tension in her shoulders and neck and lower back unfurled themselves, causing her eyes to cross beneath her heavy lids. The distant sound of a sportscast began to seem farther and farther away, then a light tap on the bathroom door brought her back around.

Mia gathered more bubbles in front of her and then called out in a friendly, mellow tone.

"Come in . . ."

"Made you that tea you wanted," Ryan said, easing into the bathroom and handing it down to her. "They had mint, Earl Grey, and chamomile . . . so I went for the one that said *relaxing* on the bag and put in one sugar. If you want more, I can bring it in?"

"No . . . this is fine," she said, taking a careful sip. "Thanks so much."

He smiled. "No, thank you. The game lasts another forty-five minutes, so take your time."

She laughed and shooed him out, flinging bubbles at him that he easily avoided.

Ryan closed the door behind him and pushed the room service tray out into the hall. The game was a great distraction; so was humor as his best defense. He'd braced himself before he'd opened the bathroom door, but there was no mental preparation that could have steeled his mind against her lacy, hot pink panties draped over the shower stall next to her bra. Just like there was no way to stop envisioning the rest of her wet, slicked, naked body beneath the bubbles in the humid bathroom. And yet he was proud of himself. He'd stuck to the plan—kept his mission focus to get in and get out without incident.

It had taken everything in him not to seek Mia's mouth when he'd bent to give her the tea. Her face was flushed from the heat of the tub, and her lush mouth was curved into an easy smile like a taunt, if not a dare. Her thick black lashes were at half-mast, giving her big brown eyes a sultry dream-like quality. Tiny bubbles teased him, popping but not fast enough, providing him a glimpse of her cleavage and the tops of her knees, but nothing more.

And damn it all if he didn't have wood just thinking about it. But here again, he was unprepared. Circumstances had put him in a dilemma—and that was probably for the best. Maybe it was a freakin' sign from God to keep his hands off the woman and stay on point. He had to believe that; otherwise it would just seem like some cruel cosmic joke.

"Watch the game, man," Ryan muttered to himself.

Bunching the pillows up at the headboard, he took a spectator's position in the middle of the bed. He'd just finish watching the highlights on ESPN, and then when Mia came back in, he could move to the chaise longue to keep things cool. But maybe he'd just rest his eyes for a moment and listen to the game. The insides of his lids felt like sandpaper when he closed his eyes.

Mia staggered out of the bathroom. Cool dry air immediately confronted her, stripping away the warm blanket of humidity that had surrounded her for almost an hour. If it hadn't been for the cup of tea she was holding and intermittently sipping, she might have slid under the surface of the water and drowned in her sleep.

As she quietly moved to her gym bag to deposit her soiled clothes, her legs were wet noodles under her weight. She stared at Ryan for a few moments, watching his chest slowly rise and fall as he rested peacefully. The poor man had to be exhausted. But she also had a healthy respect for his profession, and made a little noise just to get him to stir before she approached the bed—where a loaded gun lay on the nightstand.

"Oh, hey," he said in a groggy voice. "Didn't mean to take up the whole bed." He sat up slowly and yawned, and then swung his legs over the side with a quiet chuckle. "Well, at least I warmed it up for you."

"Please. There's enough room in there for both of us," she said, crossing the room and folding back the covers. "You need some rest and there's no way six foot four of guy is gonna squeeze up on that teeny chaise longue."

"The floor is fine, trust me. I'm so tired I could sleep standing up." Ryan clicked off the television with the remote control and slid it onto the nightstand table beside his cell phone and his gun.

Mia just shook her head. He was practically delirious. The man had fallen asleep with the remote in his hand. At least it wasn't the huge firearm. She could just envision him stirring, forgetting which gadget he had in his hand, and accidentally turning the TV off by a very permanent method.

"Nope. If you're my strong line of defense, I want you well rested and well fed, soldier," she said with a smile. "Stretch out. That's an order."

"They sent me to guard an angel of mercy," he said, allowing his body to fall back against the soft mattress.

She slipped into the bed beside him and covered them both up. "I have a wake-up call already in.

Did it right after I put in your burger order. So we're good for seven hours, and then I'll order breakfast, okay? Good night."

"Bless you," he murmured into the back of her scalp, sending warm tendrils of breath to caress it.

"Good night," she murmured, drawing herself up into a little ball on her side.

Instant heat blanketed her back as Ryan curved his body to spoon around hers. A heavy, warm hand covered her palm against her belly, capturing her arm beneath sinew and bone. Slow, steady breaths pelted the crown of her head, and it felt like a massive, muscular wall of protection had completely enveloped her. A sense of well-being filtered through her consciousness as she began to drift off to sleep. Oddly, for the first time in a very long time she felt safe. If this was the way the government sent in their special forces, well all right . . . go Army.

Dawn sent a blue-gray haze of light into the room. It amazed her that they'd both slept so soundly that she awakened in the same position that she'd been in five and a half hours ago.

The best part of it all was, Ryan was still that massive fortress of warmth at her back. His steady inhalations and exhalations created a hypnotic lull that pulled her into that semi-conscious place of nirvana. Through half-closed eyes she could see the clock on her side of the bed. She could doze for an hour and a half before the day would begin.

Mia snuggled back into the living warmth behind her and allowed her eyes to fully close. A soft sigh escaped her lips. If she were a cat, she would have purred. Soon she felt Ryan stretch a little, then resettle himself, and then kiss the back of her head gently. In reflex she released a small hum of satisfaction, allowing her feet to glide over his, which were twice the size of hers. He pulled her a little closer and breathed in her scent in a deep inhale, his hand now stroking the back of hers.

Nuzzling her hair, his body stirred. It was as though each part of him was waking up slowly, taking its own sweet time to acknowledge the morning. Another kiss warmed the back of her head. Now the lazy, haphazard stroke over the back of her palm swept a little farther up her torso, stopping just under her breasts in a way that made them ache, and then retreated to glide up and over the swell of her hip. Once sleep-sodden limbs began to awaken to tangle with hers, and the muscle in his groin pulsed to the increasing pace of his breath.

It was all so slow, so fluid, like a sensual Garden of Eden ballet. They both knew that they shouldn't test the boundaries so close to the edge, but just a little more had set things in motion at the cusp of dawn.

Floating between semi-sleep and desire, she felt lush and wet and fertile, now pliant, and his body became tense and probing, a counterbalancing flow to her ebb. Somehow during one slow, sweeping pass over her hip and thigh, her robe followed the path of his hand, exposing her flesh to the heat of his flesh. The immediate sound of him pulling his breath in sharply between his teeth made her body flood and spill more to put out his fire.

His response was a long, slow thrust against the slickness, that wet the seam of her, and that woke her up with a quiet gasp as she reached back and held his hip, pulling him in tighter. He moved her hair out of his face with an impatient shrug to press his lips against the side of her neck and then her ear. A rough-hewn hand captured her now exposed breast, gently thumbing her nipple to the same lazy rhythm of his nonpenetrating stroke.

The message was clear: She set the boundaries, and she made the rules. Although his breaths shuddered now, she knew he wouldn't enter her, but had left the hard choice for her. Needing to feel him deeper, she arched, her backside now welded to his pelvis, the contractions within her canal causing her entire body to ache.

The abrupt change in her tempo and pressure dredged a low moan up from his diaphragm. She felt the deep resonant vibration though her back, through her spine, through her womb as he shifted, still trying to make the decision hers, but holding her tightly around the waist, a knee beginning to part her thighs. His shallow breaths were a silent plea-chant . . . *Let me know. Oh, God . . . Please, let me know.*

But somewhere deep within her, she didn't want to be responsible for handing him the apple. Surely, they both knew it was wrong, unwise, crazy even, to go into something this hot unprotected. But it was also five-something-A.M. And Lord knew it was so freakin' hot. Ten years was a murder sentence, and they'd both done hard time.

His hand slipped between her thighs, the tip of a long agile finger found her bud . . . and that made her find her voice to say his name.

Just one word breathed out in agony set off a chain reaction of him repeatedly knocking at the door of where it now hurt so badly. Each hard thrust was punctuated by his moan as he pulled back just to hit her opening again without entering. So close and yet so far; she couldn't take it any longer and captured him within her on the next pass, a hard back-thrust to explain her decision with authority, no words needed.

His body seized as he groaned out her name fused with that of the Almighty. Just feeling him lodged within her to the hilt brought back instant muscle memory that contracted her pelvic floor, her very core, and made her throw her head back to buck beneath him hard and fast.

One hand against the headboard, the other gripped around her waist, his thrusts lifted them both off the bed, sweat coursing down his arm, wet heat singeing her back. She felt herself topple over the edge of the first orgasm with a jerky spasm, but as his built, the strokes got longer, more deliberate, until he froze for a second and then let it go.

Wave after wave of spasmodic pleasure connected them like they'd both tripped over a live wire. Dropping against the mattress, he turned her closer toward him and kissed her hard with tears in his eyes.

"I couldn't help it," he admitted in a deep rasp. "I just couldn't help it."

She traced the sweat rolling down his temple with a shaking finger. "Neither could I."

Still breathing hard, he withdrew from her with a wince and turned her fully toward him, then lowered his forehead to rest against hers with his eyes closed.

Mia closed her eyes tightly. She was not trying to trap the man . . . this wasn't supposed to go down like this. Yeah, she could have stopped it, could have gotten up. Not only did they bite the danged apple, they ate that sucker whole and swallowed the seeds.

"You okay?" she murmured, stroking the nape of his neck. "What are you thinking?"

"Nothing righteous, I promise you."

She swallowed hard, not sure how to take what he meant. "Okay."

"For real?" He pulled back and looked at her. Clear agony was in his expression.

"Yeah . . . it's okay," she said, touching his cheek,

trying to convey that she understood how he felt. This was pretty messed up.

He kissed her slowly and did a one-handed push-up over her body, gathering her weight in the other hand, palming her ass until she was again joined to him. Catching on, she wrapped her legs around his waist to make the seal unbreakable, and then laughed quietly, slowly understanding that what he'd been thinking and what she'd been worrying about were two vastly different things.

"We already messed up once," she murmured, trying to wrest clarity back after the fact.

"Yeah I know . . . but since we did . . ."

She held him tighter around the neck. "If I get pregnant, you know it's all your fault."

"Uh-huh . . . ," he murmured. Slowly guiding them off the bed and standing with her while inside her. "I'll take all the blame."

"You gonna marry me?" she teased as he began walking them toward the bathroom.

"Yeah . . . shoulda done that a long time ago."

"Stop playing." She rested her forehead in the crook of his neck.

"Who's playing," he murmured, kissing her neck and opening the bathroom door.

She looked up at him. "Focus, man . . . do you know what you're saying and why we're here in the first place?"

"I am focused," he murmured with a smirk. "I'm

Delta Force and can walk and chew gum at the same time . . . last I checked, I just asked you to marry me and all damned night I was thinking about me and you in that glass shower, girl. I think the pink panties just stuck in my mind . . . Now get in here."

CHAPTER 17

Ryan crossed the street and climbed into the black GMC. Ken was waiting for him. He kept Mia in his line of vision at the cab stand outside the hotel while Dr. Cortland chatted with her, oblivious that he was there or even existed. Leaving her had been the hardest fifteen minutes of his life. Every fiber within him said to stay close. But if he did that, he'd alert Cortland, and possibly put her in greater danger by having her around another panicky civilian.

"Just one question, man," Ken said in a tone that made Ryan look at him.

Ken's expression brightened into a beaming smile. "How'd you sleep?"

"Don't even go there," Ryan said, shaking his head and trying not to laugh.

"I just wanna know why I got to stake out the hotel entrance keeping watch on an eighty-six-year-old man with night-vision goggles while the temperatures dropped, and had to eat freeze-dried MREs for dinner, and then finally got to sleep for five minutes standing up? Whereas, other people who shall remain nameless . . . hey. I can only speculate. Just a question."

"Because, *Lieutenant,* you shouldn't speculate." Ryan lifted his chin and swallowed a smile as he returned his gaze across the street.

"I ain't mad at you, Captain," Ken said in awe. "In fact, my new nickname for you is gonna be Bond, James Bond."

"Nah," Ryan said with a sheepish grin. "That was another lifetime. Bond doesn't fit a married man."

"What?" Ken leaned in and put the back of his hand on Ryan's forehead, and Ryan playfully slapped it away. "We've got a situation, sir! Man down! I need an extraction, stat—copy!"

"Man, shut up," Ryan said, laughing.

"Did I hear you right?"

Ryan nodded. "Shoulda did it ten years ago, man."

"No, what you shoulda did was stay out here in the elements—in the ass-biting cold—to keep your head clear."

Ryan laughed hard and pointed a forefinger at Ken. "Mind your business, Lieutenant—and that's an order."

"Yes, sir—just looking out for my best homeboy. Damn . . ."

"What I really need you to do is look out for my future wife."

Ken extended a hand to Ryan and shook it, pulling him in for a brief man-hug. "I'm happy for you, dude. Seriously. If you like it, I love it. You ain't never been right since y'all split anyway."

"Thanks, man. But we're gonna have to break it to Ethan real easy."

Ken leaned his head back and laughed. "Yeah. Our boy is a piece of work!"

All joking ceased as a cab came up and collected Mia and Dr. Cortland. It was back to business. Ryan shifted the vehicle into drive and pulled out trailing the taxi. The plan was simple. She'd get on the Acela with Dr. Cortland. He'd already been cleared to get on after all the passengers—Amtrak officials would tell the conductor to hold for a security detail. No problem.

An incoming MI call over Ryan's encrypted cell phone drew both men's attention.

"Captain Mason?"

"Affirmative. Stand by. I'm putting you on speaker so Lieutenant Christopher can hear. Copy." Ryan tossed his cell phone to Ken to hold as he navigated the road.

"Roger that. We've been analyzing the break-in attempt hits to Dr. Austin's online database subscriptions that involve her research, as well as the remote access attempts to the systems in her office. It had to be someone who knew her very well. They knew every permutation of her birthday, her mother's birthday, sibling names, pet names, graduation dates, class rank, et cetera. Some of those things you could search by looking up details she has on Facebook and other social networking sites or in public docs that are out there. However, even with all of that, Dr. Austin has been very spartan about her personal data on the Web. But what makes us wonder if this was a close friend or colleague is that within hours of her going public, the hacks started, with surprising accuracy on her personal data. Nicknames, pet names, really personal stuff that wasn't in the news or readily available online."

"Were any of the hacks successful?" Ryan said, gripping the wheel tighter.

"No. But the data set she chose to password-protect her data is interesting, sir. We hacked it."

"Clarify."

"It was your graduation date from West Point, your birthday, and your mother's address in Brooklyn, sir. Enemy hackers went away frustrated . . . but, uhmm . . . her detailed knowledge of you is a little uncanny."

Ken and Ryan shared a look.

Avoiding the unspoken question, Ryan pushed on for relevant data. "Any prints, leads, anything to go on regarding the break-in at her apartment?"

"Just one weird thing, sir. The door was busted off the hinges, but there was also a key broken in the lock. It was as though someone tried an old key and then it snapped in the door—that's when they decided to get in the old-fashioned way."

"And of course the downstairs neighbors didn't hear a thing."

"No, because according to the elderly woman who lives on the floor below, she was given a dinner coupon to use because the super was supposed to fumigate the building for a few hours. All she said was some African guy wearing maintenance duds told her to leave and gave her the coupon. So she did."

"You got a description from her, I take it?"

"Yeah. Generic as hell, though."

Ryan could feel his teeth grinding.

"Have our men in New York pick up and lean on one Dr. David Williams for some information. He's at the conference that Dr. Austin and Dr. Cortland are returning to."

"Roger that. Relationship, if any, to the assets?"

"Williams was once employed by Dr. Cortland and is the ex-fiancé of Dr. Austin."

"Roger."

"Out here," Ryan said, and then took the phone from Ken and ended the call.

"What I'm about to say is not a challenge of your authority, just an observation," Ken said in a careful tone. "If you lean on this civilian without probable cause, it's going to look extremely questionable to the brass once you announce that you're getting married. I've got your back, but I just wanna be sure your lines aren't getting blurry. If you're wrong, this sort of thing can be a career killer."

"I'm clear as a bell, Lieutenant—and if I'm right, failure to act could kill *her*." Ryan swerved the car to follow the cab that seemed to have sped up. "Listen, man . . . I know how this looks, but he left the Smithsonian disgruntled about being passed over. He no doubt once had a key to Mia's apartment. I'm sure he would have known all sorts of intimate facts about her."

"True. And our boys with the big eye in the sky said you dropped him in a street behind the hotel while you had supermarket bags in your hand and your arm around the lady." Ken rubbed his chin and stared at Ryan hard. "I'm not trying to be a pain in your ass; I've got your back, man—you know I'm watching your six. But just be really sure you have things clearly sorted out before we go traumatizing some dude who'll be writing his congressman and trying to sue."

Mia tucked away any annoyance she felt when she and Dr. Cortland got into the cab and she recognized she'd gotten the slacker again. Of all the freakin' cabs in DC, she had to get the guy with the attitude. But nothing was going to ruin the way she felt today. After the morning she'd spent with Ryan . . . and the man had *proposed*—albeit with a little prompting. But still.

It was all so sudden, so crazy and intense. Yet

that was the nature of what they'd always shared. After ten years and traveling around the world, the guy comes home and makes up his mind just like that—in two days? She smiled and sent her gaze out the window, temporarily forgetting that she was even in the vehicle with Dr. Cortland and the cabdriver.

"My dear, your mind has been drifting in and out of our conversation since we met in the lobby."

"Oh, I am so sorry . . . I'm just—oh I don't know what. Discombobulated."

Mia shook her head and laughed at herself, wishing she could just blurt out the good news, knowing that her mother, sister, and Camille were going to scream their heads off when she called.

"*Discombobulated* sums it up quite accurately," Dr. Cortland said with a wink. "And no need to apologize. I was your age once, and the thrill of success and getting true recognition for your work can cause for sleepless nights and some very foggy days."

"I'll be fine, sir, and thank you for understanding." Mia let out a quiet sigh of relief, because for a moment she wasn't sure if Dr. Cortland had seen Ryan and had recognized him.

But as she glimpsed Dr. Cortland from the corner of her eye, he seemed nonplussed. Hopefully her secret rendezvous was safe.

"Well, all this business makes me weary, at my age. I'm sure you'll also be glad to be home and just sleep in your own bed."

Mia caught the cabdriver's eyes in his rearview. He'd clearly been gleaning bits and pieces of their conversation. Staying in character to not upset Dr. Cortland, she followed Ryan's advice.

"Oh, yeah, I am really looking forward to getting a good night's sleep at home."

The cabbie's eyes remained strangely on hers. Totally rude.

"So are you coming right back?" Dr. Cortland asked in a chipper tone.

"No . . . I was thinking of staying through the weekend to visit my mom and returning on Sunday." Mia continued to lock gazes with the cabdriver. Something about the guy's intense interest in their conversation was giving her the creeps.

"Oh, I bet she'll like that. You'll be in for some home cooking."

"Yeah . . . ," Mia murmured, and then suddenly didn't want to discuss her family and how much they meant to her around the stranger who was driving the cab.

A vague fear made her glance away and quickly out the back window in search of Ryan's vehicle. It was there, lumbering along at a leisurely pace behind them. But no sooner did she turn back than the cab lurch as the cabbie pressed down on the accelerator.

"Now see here!" Dr. Cortland fussed, holding on to the seat as the cab jumped a light and careened through traffic. "What is the meaning of this? You stop this cab this—"

"Shut up, old man!" the cabbie yelled, whipping out a large nickel-plated gun from under his seat and pointing it at Dr. Cortland.

Mia grabbed Dr. Cortland and hugged him against her, trying to quiet the elderly man before he got himself killed.

"You do exactly as I say and you will not be hurt. We need what's in your mind, not to have brains splattered all over the car. Understood?"

Mia and Dr. Cortland nodded, and he squeezed her hand tightly, his face beet red from fear and outrage.

"Good." The cabbie drew back and placed the weapon on the seat beside him. He slowed down slightly, enough to look like a normal cab breaking traffic rules in a major city. "Now call your cop friend and tell him to back off."

The cabbie looked over his shoulder at Mia when she didn't move. "Don't play stupid. We will kill the old man if you do not cooperate. But we know about this cop of yours. So call him and tell him you do not need him at the train station."

"What is this all about, Mia?" Dr. Cortland asked, but the question brought the barrel of the gun over the seat and pointed at his face again.

Mia quickly rifled through her purse, got out her cell phone, and punched in Ryan's number. As soon as the call connected, she began talking quickly, not allowing Ryan to say something that could give him away or get them killed, and hoping with all her might that he'd get the real message through the strain in her tone.

"I don't need you at the train station, okay," she said. "In fact, I don't want you to crowd me and my mentor. Just back off—I'm sick of you following me and making me paranoid about bullshit that doesn't exist. We clear? Good. Have a nice day."

"Give me the phone," the cabbie said with a sneer and then looked at Dr. Cortland. "If you have one, too, don't be foolish."

Ryan listened to the dead line for two seconds and hit speed dial, accelerating behind the speeding cab. He didn't have time to process fear or rage; everything he'd been trained to do all his adult life kicked in on pure instinct.

"Enemy engaged—with civilian assets as hostages in a commercial vehicle, a yellow cab, license plate—I spell: Victor, Romeo, Alpha, Tango, Three, Four. Copy. We are in hot pursuit," Ryan said, flinging his phone to Ken, who caught it and then checked the magazine on his weapon.

"I copy, Delta. Go to secure channel."

Ken immediately opened up a secure channel on the radio in the glove compartment. "Situation hot! Copy. Target just made a right onto 9th Street heading due south toward the I-395 Beltway."

"Roger that, we have GPS directional."

"We suspect they are heading to the train station, but cannot confirm," Ryan shouted.

"We'll put a bird in the sky, Delta."

"Negative!"

"Say again?"

"Negative. The hostage called; the enemy is spooked. Fall back—this extraction is delicate—like threading the needle. Keep a visual at a distance. We need to know if they exit on Louisiana Avenue heading northwest toward Columbus Circle, or northeast if their destination is the train station. We'll take an alternate route through the city and need a pickup and air traffic clearance. What's the closest building that has a helipad?"

"We'll be on standby, Delta. We'll have a bird waiting for you on top of the National Air and Space Museum. Copy."

"Roger. Out here," Ryan said, and then Ken clicked off the radio just as Ryan's cell phone rang.

Pulling away from hot pursuit to go in for a more strategic maneuver that wouldn't spook Mia's kidnappers, Ryan swerved their vehicle into a hard left on 7th Street, barreling through traffic toward Independence Avenue. Police vehicles instantly scrambled and cleared a path while Ken answered the incoming call on Ryan's encrypted cell phone.

"Captain Mason—our boys combed the hotel. Found Dr. David Williams beaten to death with a

DO NOT DISTURB sign on his door. That probably rules him out as an active source."

"That doesn't rule him out," Ryan said, careening onto Independence Avenue with a hard stop. He and Ken jumped out of the vehicle and rushed up the steps, only to be met by guards who had an elevator to the roof waiting. "Check cell phone records, email correspondence, and pull bank records. He wouldn't be the first guy to sell information and then get burned. We want to know if he was talking to anybody."

"Roger that."

CHAPTER 18

He'd left her? From the risked quick glimpse behind her she saw that, as their cab barreled onto I-395, Ryan's vehicle had stopped short and swerved away like a jilted lover.

The cabdriver smiled in the rearview mirror with smug satisfaction. Mia gathered Dr. Cortland closer, trying to quiet and comfort the elderly man as though he were a frightened child. As much as she was afraid for her own safety, she was terrified for his. It was obvious that they needed something specific from her, while they needed nothing but blood from him. Her beloved mentor had only been brought along to leverage her. They could torture and kill him right before her eyes to extract the information they needed.

Yet she knew full well that if she cooperated and gave them what they wanted—the parts of her presentation that she didn't make public, the parts that showed exact coordinates of where to detonate explosives to create a catastrophic event—then what? Both she and Dr. Cortland were dead.

Her mind scrambled for answers as the taxi barreled around Columbus Circle, bypassed Union Station, and entered the large concrete parking garage behind it. Spiraling upward, going from floor to floor, the cab finally came to a stop.

"Get out," the gunman ordered, then jumped out and opened Mia's door, half dragging her to her feet.

From out of nowhere a tall, black man wearing an army jacket over jeans and an orange-and-green embroidered shirt came up behind them and grabbed Dr. Cortland. Within seconds he'd yanked the old man into his hold and forced a white cloth over his face. Dr. Cortland slumped. Mia twisted to scream an objection, but the gunman leveled his revolver at her temple. The tall black man threw the cloth aside and lugged Dr. Cortland's limp body to another parked vehicle while Mia watched helplessly in horror.

"Just to make him sleep quietly," the gunman said, removing the weapon from Mia's head. "You give us what we need and he'll wake up in a parking lot somewhere safe. You don't; he won't. Simple."

A hard grip on her arm yanked her forward toward a van with dark windows. From the corner of her eye she saw the homeless man who was a Union Station fixture pushing his cart and trying to hide from parking lot security. Other cars passed by, people eager to get to work or their destinations. But no one stopped, except the man with nothing but time on his hands.

"Hey, nice lady—can you help a brother out?" The homeless man beamed at her as he called out from a distance.

"Fuck off, you homeless trash!" the cabdriver shouted, shoving Mia forward but concealing his weapon. "Go get a job!"

"You stay blessed, too," the homeless man said in a churlish tone. "Asshole!"

Mia stumbled into the van as the door opened from the inside and an angry shove hit her back. She fell against the seat with a thud that knocked the wind out of her lungs.

Inside were two men wearing inexpensive, ill-fitting business suits. One was very fair and had a full beard; the other was darker, ruddier in hue, clean-cut, and could have passed for an Ivy League student. But the unmistakable element that defined both men was that they both had guns.

"Put this on and cover yourself," the student-looking gunman ordered. Becoming impatient with Mia's fumbling, he snatched the large swath of fabric and threw it over her head. "Your hair—cover it, whore."

The chopper set down on an adjacent building. If they had set down on the roof of the parking lot, just the sound of the rotor could trigger a desperate action by the enemy. As long as Mia was in their grasp, there was no room for errors.

In a flat-out dash, Ryan and Ken skirted pedestrian traffic and headed up the ramp of the garage. Amtrak security was now on high alert. The base of the parking lot was secured for any exiting vehicles. All exits from the parking lot into the station or out to the street were being monitored. But the way Ryan saw it, that still left too much room for error.

Rounding the second level, Ryan and Ken frantically scanned the concrete-and-metal horizon. Normal activity meant nothing, yet searching for Mia in a huge uncontained space was like looking for a needle in a haystack. No doubt the enemy had changed vehicles. They could have already exited with her concealed on the floor or in the trunk. If his calculated risk didn't pan out and he'd somehow allowed her to slip through the cracks, there would be no forgiving himself.

He'd almost dropped the homeless dude who'd come out from between two parked cars and knew he had to get calmer, had to bring his involvement away from the personal and back to the laser focus that detachment provided.

"Everybody jumpy and mean today . . . and ain't nobody tryin'ta bless ol' LeRoy. That ain't right," the homeless man argued as Ryan sidestepped him and jogged down the aisle. "Even my pretty lady acting all stank—don't speak 'cause she gots a new man. Fuck her, too! Even though I loves her."

Half of what the homeless man said bounced off Ryan's eardrums from sheer adrenaline. The other half of it stuck somewhere deep in the recesses of his street wisdom: The unseen always see everything.

He rushed back to the man and pulled out some bills. Ken ran down another aisle and looked back at Ryan with confusion.

"Man, I'ma bless you today if you tell me about the pretty lady."

LeRoy grabbed the bills in a dirty fist and smiled, looking at Ryan with bloodshot eyes. "She hurt my feelings, man. Last time she at least spoke like I was a human being. But today she was wit' some asshole who was pushing her around. He had the nerve to tell me to get a job."

"Do you know what their car looked like?"

LeRoy counted his bills, smiling with brown teeth as he realized there were a few twenties mixed in with a couple of fives. "Man . . . she got in a dark blue van with some cats who was changing clothes and probably getting their freak on in there before she got there. People be nasty these days, all out in the street wit' dey bizness."

"How many? Was she with an old man?"

Henry looked up at Ryan and then suddenly frowned. "You a cop, right? Got a cop look and asking cop questions. And I might be's mad at my fine lady, but I ain't turning her in. Ol' LeRoy don't snitch."

Just like that, the conversation was over. LeRoy began pushing his cart and mumbling about the indignities of the world. Ken had stopped his search, his gaze fixed on Ryan, waiting for a signal to move. Ryan jogged beside LeRoy and pulled out another twenty.

"I'm not trying to take her down. I want her pimp so she doesn't get beat up tonight."

A crusty hand reached for the bill as LeRoy brought his cart and muttering to a halt. He gave Ryan a skeptical scowl, and then released a weary sigh.

"You never can tell about womens, you know. Naw. The old man got sick and went with that tall African brother who works as a Red Cap—thinking he high and mighty 'cause he got a good job. Fuck Abdulla! Naw, she was wit' the youngish one who was rushing her, the cabbie. Then they got in with them two in the van, and next thing I seent was her clothes was coming off. I had to leave, 'cuz I thought she was a nice sister, you know. She seemed clean like a schoolteacher, or something. I ain't know that's how she made her money—but who am I? I'm not judging a chile of the Lord. And this is DC. But I couldn't watch all that. The shit was blowing my high."

"Thanks," Ryan said, turning to look across the

lot at Ken. "Remember what level they were on and how long ago?"

LeRoy shrugged and began walking. "Almost to the top and maybe five, ten minutes ago—but don't hol' me to it. I ain't so good 'bout time."

Ryan ran over to Ken, his cell phone already in hand, sending information into it in short bursts while on the move.

"Blue van. Coming down the ramps. Primary asset has been forced to change clothes. Interior van—three armed targets. Secondary asset may be injured and has been separated from primary. Identify target, name: Abdulla—employee of Amtrak Red Cap service. Out."

Moderate traffic filed down the ramp as they took concealed positions between parked cars. Finally a dark blue mini van with tinted side windows passed. Through the approaching van's windshield, Ryan could see that a woman wearing a burqa sat in the backseat. Two men were in the front seats. One was next to the driver, making that two easy shots through the windows. The difficult one would be the one next to the woman. But the problem was identification. He had to have a positive ID. He couldn't fire on potentially innocent civilians based on a very loose description by a half-crazy homeless addict.

The only way to be sure would be to do something completely insane: an old-fashioned carjacking. It was the best attempt he could make to confuse the targets into hesitating for a second to process whether or not he was just doing what sometimes went down in the city. That would be far less dangerous for Mia than if they thought otherwise. He knew that if they believed he was just a thug and not the police, they would shoot at him, not Mia. And if they were civilians, they'd panic and comply. Either way he'd find out in two seconds what he was dealing with to avoid firing on friendlies.

Running out into the open in front of the van, Ryan rounded the vehicle and grabbed hold of the driver's-side door, running with the moving car.

"Gimme the van and the cash!" he shouted, pointing his M1911 at the driver's head through the open window.

Ken was on the other door in a heartbeat, running alongside the vehicle. Then it all happened in slow motion.

The driver lifted a Glock nine-millimeter at the same time the man in the back with Mia lifted an AK-47. The passenger spun on Ken with a sawed-off shotgun. Mia ducked her head and screamed. The pitch of her voice could have shattered glass. The van instantly lurched toward a concrete column, with Ryan between the van and the column. He squeezed off two shots—the first blowing the side of the driver's skull off, the second a single shot through the window taking out the assailant who had been holding Mia. A burst of machine-gun fire ripped through the side of the van as Mia's captor fell. Ryan jumped back and rolled between two parked cars to avoid being crushed in the column crash. Ken unloaded four shots into the passenger-side target as his pump shotgun blasted a hole in the floor of the van.

Ryan scrambled beneath parked cars to get out in the open. Ken had his weapon trained on the smoking, crashed vehicle. Ryan flung open the passenger-side door and yanked out a dead body. Both men got the doors open, clearing a path to Mia. Ryan reached her first, and pulled back the black fabric, praying to God that Mia was under it.

CHAPTER 19

Strong hands pulled her beyond the horror of blood splatter and gore. The smell of death and broken bowels made her heave and lose her breakfast on the parking garage ground the moment she exited the van. Carnage was everywhere. Wet, blood-soaked fabric was ripped from her body and she gasped for air as she was lifted away from vomit and another dead man on the ground.

She fell into Ryan's arms trembling so badly that her entire body hurt. Familiar safe arms surrounded her, crushing her to his chest. In the very distant corner of her mind, she heard another deep male voice barking orders in short bursts. His words stabbed into her brain and made her head throb. Ryan was asking her questions at the same time that the big burly guy behind him was saying something about getting a containment team in to seal down the area . . . sweepers to clean up the mess. Then his words, "Primary asset acquired, secondary still with enemy at large," reminded her that Dr. Cortland was still missing.

"We have to find him," Mia said, looking up from Ryan's chest. "They took Ian!"

"That's what I'm asking," Ryan said, holding her firmly by her upper arms. "Give me something to go on—what type of vehicle?"

"Tan . . . old," she said, squeezing her eyes shut tightly. "An old Chevy Malibu."

"Copy that," the man behind Ryan said.

Then they began running with Ryan's arm around her. They took the ramp, the other guy able to get farther, faster, without her as a burden. But Ryan was on his cell phone in seconds, holding it with one hand and shouting commands into it while he ushered her forward next to him with the other.

At the bottom of the ramp they met a phalanx of unmarked vans and police cruisers. Ryan made a quick motion with his hand, calling over a uniformed officer, and then barked out a command.

"Take this package to the Pentagon."

"Yes, sir," the officer replied.

As she was handed off and Ryan ran forward, she saw a homeless guy yelling and throwing cans at Ryan yelling, "Traitor!"

There was no time to figure out the insanity. An efficient officer had her by the elbow and was helping her into a car.

"Ma'am, it's gonna be all right. Just come with us."

"Get this bird in the air, Lieutenant!" Ryan shouted over the chopper din.

The aircraft lifted off and pulled out over the teeming city streets below.

"What've we got?" Ryan shouted, looking at Ken.

"One Abdullah Hijaz is living down in Southeast DC with his sister who came here eight years ago from Liberia. Her Sudanese husband owns a grocery store. We've got the tags on the vehicle because in order to park as an employee Hijaz had to register it with Amtrak. We've got three birds in the sky, ground team in cruisers looking for it on the street. The vehicle left the lot fifteen minutes before our raid, per the time stamp on the exit gate—he used his employee monthly card to get out."

"Damn!"

"I know, Captain."

The radio in the chopper squawked, and both Ryan and Ken put on the padded headphones.

"We tracked cell phone activity in a flurry as late as yesterday between the deceased Dr. Williams and one Dr. Joshua Lewis—also a colleague of Dr. Austin."

"Where is Lewis now?" Ryan glanced at Ken.

"We've detained him at Dulles, trying to catch

a flight to the Bahamas, sir. We're in the process of pulling his bank records now, just as we are on Williams—looking for any large transfers or deposits."

"Roger," Ryan said. "Good job. Now just get me some intel on Hijaz's address and the closest location to it that we can set this bird down."

As soon as the open lot came into view, Ryan motioned for the pilot to set the chopper down. Exiting quickly, he and Ken ducked low as the helicopter lifted off again. He could see the car that had the hostage, but they had to get the chopper away from a possible blast if the trunk was wired. Breathing hard as much from the jog as the anxiety, he and Ken shared a look. This could go very, very bad or very, very good.

Dr. Cortland gasped and tried to open his eyes.

His head throbbed and his stomach roiled with nausea. Oppressive heat made him gag as sweat caused his clothes to feel like second skin. Suddenly he was aware that although his eyes were open, he couldn't see. Nor could he stretch out his arms and legs. He was entombed in an uncomfortable metal prison. He could smell dust and sour mildew and a heavy petroleum scent that he couldn't identify. He could also hear children playing at some game that drew rowdy cheers when he strained to listen. Traffic.

But heavy bricks weighed him down. He didn't

understand, couldn't see. Then suddenly there were angry men's voices. Shots were fired. Now the children's voices were gone. They had killed children? Dear God, no . . .

Wherever he was began rocking. Then there was a pop, then a whoosh, air flooding in with a bright flash of light. Thick hands and strong arms were pulling him forward, running with him. The yelling began in earnest as he began falling forward and the air seemed to suck away from the earth to be replaced by a world-shattering *kaboom*.

Mia sat with a cup of coffee and a cup of water before her, ignoring it, sucking on a mint. Her ID and purse had been recovered, but until Ryan and Dr. Cortland came back, nothing else mattered.

"Ma'am, anything more that you can tell us will aid us not only in continuing to protect you, but also in keeping your loved ones safe."

Mia stared across the table at the man who'd asked her the question. She didn't know if he was military, Secret Service, FBI, a police detective, or what. All the branches of government ran together with her tears. "Did they find him?" she asked.

"Who, ma'am?"

"Dr. Cortland. Did they find Ian?"

"I'm not at liberty to discuss an ongoing investigation, ma'am. You will be informed of an update when we have clearance to do so."

Mia closed her eyes. "Is my momma all right?

Has anybody checked on her to be sure they didn't try to take her? They put chloroform on Ian's face and I saw how easily they can take people. I have a brother . . . a sister, nieces and nephews. Oh, God, Camille! She's right here in DC!"

"Ma'am . . . we're gonna do our job. Now we need you to give us every bit of information about people who might have been interested in your work so we can make sure the worst doesn't happen."

The blast from the wired trunk was a few seconds late. That was the only thing that saved them— botched timing.

Ryan was deaf for what felt like nearly twenty minutes and still heard church bells inside his head. The concussion of the blast had put him, Ken, and Dr. Cortland facedown, partially behind a concrete street barrier and abandoned cars, eating junkyard dirt. The old man didn't stir. Ryan glanced around; thankfully no children were anywhere to be found. The shots they fired were enough to scatter the ragtag soccer team. Ryan let his breath out slowly and began to feel a knifing pain in his side. He placed his hand against it and it came away warm and wet . . . he didn't have to look to know what it was. Just before he collapsed he noticed where a section of the Malibu's bumper was lodged. It had blown off the car that detonated and caught him in the side.

* * *

A federal agent sat on the edge of the desk in the airport holding room. The two TSA agents who had asked Dr. Joshua Lewis to step out of line were dismissed and replaced by a phalanx of grim-looking Secret Service men.

"I know my rights," Josh said. "I want an attorney and—"

"Under the Patriot Act, you can be detained indefinitely for acts of terrorism," the agent said, calmly brushing invisible lint off his navy-blue jacket sleeves. He looked up at Josh with hard gray eyes. "Five . . . ten years could go by before we even remember where your cell is in Gitmo."

"The president is shutting that facility down!" Josh said, fidgeting. He was about to stand and then thought better of it when two agents just shook their heads slowly as though that would be a bad idea.

"He is . . . but the wheels of justice and change move slowly. Could take a few years, so maybe my guesstimate of five to ten being lost in the system was inaccurate." The lead agent stood and fastened a button on his jacket.

"But I didn't do anything wrong!" Josh said, his panicked gaze now ricocheting from face to face.

"You've been having a lot of conversations with Dr. David Williams all of a sudden . . . that concerns people."

"And how is that a crime, huh? We used to be colleagues."

"It becomes a crime when Dr. Williams's and your bank accounts mysteriously increase the same day someone tries to break into Dr. Mia Austin's office and home to steal her research." The agent nodded as Josh's eyes widened. "Get him on a flight to Guantanamo, gentlemen. I don't have time for this bullshit."

"No—wait, wait, listen. I was just the broker."

The agent stopped by the door. Josh nervously dragged his fingers through his hair.

"Okay, I used to know this guy . . . well, still know this guy, in grad school."

"Got a name for this guy?"

"Yeah . . . Omar Kalzemi. A rich kid. Foreigner. Smart as hell, rich as hell . . . already had an MBA from Stanford and was now slumming in the sciences and taking geology because his father was in the oil business. You know, the economy is bad, right?"

"Yeah, heard all about it on CNN," one of the agents behind the lead agent muttered.

"Well, this guy . . . he was always a little eccentric but partied big whenever he came to town." Josh looked around, blinking quickly. "We were all having a blast in his condo down in Annapolis after we'd been out all day on his yacht, when he asked if some of the far-out theories he'd heard about geological warfare and natural disaster warfare had any merit. We figured it was the coke talking when he said he'd pay big money for anything that looked credible, because he wanted to be sure his father's installations were safe over in the Middle East. It wasn't until he mentioned it again a few days later on the phone that I realized he was serious."

Josh wiped the sweat from his brow with the back of his palm. "It was crackpot science, and everybody knew it. Hell, David left the Smithsonian because he'd been passed over for that load of bull—I'd been passed over, too. But I had to stay. David had family with connections and could save face. So we were crying in our beer about it after work one night, and we got shitfaced and were joking about selling Mia's crap research to Omar for a couple million dollars to take the sting out of the career blues."

Poker-faced agents stared back at Josh without a change of expression.

"Come on, guys," Josh said, beginning to make the nail he was picking at bleed. "It was just supposed to be an exchange of nothing research for a little cash. Well, okay, a lot of cash. But *all I did* was get David in front of Omar, because David was the one who knew Mia. He used to be engaged to her, still had a key to her apartment . . . knew her passwords and whatever—hell, he used to sleep with the woman and had an ax to grind. Who knew her research really had any merit? But David did it. *He* was the one who gave Omar the information and the key, not me. After that, we were both out of it. Omar had to send in his own people to actually go get Mia's research—neither me nor David was stupid enough to actually go *steal* something."

"Really, Dr. Lewis?" the lead agent said, coming to the desk to lean down into Josh's face. "Funny thing is, your buddy David—who you just threw under the bus—is dead."

"What!" Josh was on his feet. "But, but, David and I were gonna go down there and party with Omar—this was like a big joke . . . we were gonna collect the other half of the money when Omar got the call that David's info had panned out. Why is David dead? I don't understand! Who killed David?"

The lead agent put a firm hand on his shoulder and slammed Joshua back into the chair, not immediately answering his question. "Accessory to murder, sedition, terrorism, treason—I could go on and on and spin this case against you five ways from Sunday. Ol' Omar was obviously cleaning up his trail, and the only reason your dumb ass is alive is because we picked you up in the airport. Otherwise you'd probably be swimming with the fishes in the Bahamas."

"No, swimming with the fishes—that's the Mafia's style," another agent said with an angry smirk. "These Middle East boys are more theatrical. They like C-4 and old-school message murders, like cutting off a guy's head."

"Right, right, my apologies. What was I thinking?" the lead agent said, then turned back to Joshua to get up close in his face. "My suggestion is that you give me every known way to contact your buddy Omar. I wanna know what the rich little snot drives, the name of his boat, where he keeps it docked, girlfriends, condos, whatever we need to know fast—or you're going down so hard you'll forget what daylight looks like."

In International waters off the coast
of the Bahamas . . .

"Weapons hot, target on lock," the F-16 pilot confirmed into the secure radio channel.

"Red Wolf, what's the status of potential collateral damage in the area? Do you have a visual? Our satellites are showing several clicks between this vessel and any commercial or private vessels."

"Affirmative, Colonel. All clear."

"Well, this ain't the Love Boat," Colonel Mitchell said. "No female civilians on the vessel at this time, according to our eye in the sky. All chatter is from male enemy targets."

"Waiting on your order, sir."

"Fire at will."

Ethan adjusted the wire in his ear. Chatter from Omar Kalzemi's contact back to Kalzemi put his target in motion on the aerial Roosevelt Island Tramway with Dr. Austin's laptop in his possession. With the actual hard drive that the enemy had stolen from her empty hotel room at the Marriott, hacking in would be a cinch. His orders were simple—take out the target with minimal collateral damage and recover the laptop.

Hunkering down at the apex of the steel beams above the East River that connected Roosevelt Island to Manhattan, Ethan kept his eye on the moving glass-enclosed tram. Another one would be coming in fifteen minutes, but so long as two didn't pass at the same time to block his vantage point he was good to go.

Beneath him was a 250-foot drop, and the shot that he squeezed off from his sniper's rifle would have to be as accurate as hell. Each tram traveled a distance of 3,100 feet in four and a half minutes, roughly sixteen miles per hour. His compensation for wind velocity had to be just right, or else he could take out one of the 125 passengers the tram could hold. But he had a picture in his head, one that had been downloaded to his phone. He knew what this target looked like and what he planned to do.

As soon as the man was in Ethan's sights, he released a single shell that never even shattered the glass. The boys at the other end could bag and tag the body and make sure nobody fled the car with the laptop. Now the hard part was climbing back down.

* * *

Ryan could hear voices and began to awaken, but he felt drowsy then confined, as though he were suffocating. He slowly raised his hand to his face, scrabbling at tubes. He was in the hospital? Damn. The last thing he remembered was jumping out of a chopper, running across an old junkyard lot, and dragging his target away from the vehicle with Ken. Then, *kaboom.*

"Easy, easy," a gentle voice murmured, stopping his panic and taking up his hand.

Disoriented, he slowly opened his eyes to see Mia looking down at him, with Ken and Ethan at the foot of his bed. Ethan was pacing, a bundle of nerves; Ken was standing on crutches looking worried as hell. Mia brushed his forehead with a light kiss as two big tears ran down the bridge of her nose to wet his face. Then she wiped at the dampness she'd left on his skin with shaky fingers.

"So you decided to just be a human shield and take a car bumper to the gut, rather than just dive behind a concrete junkyard barrier?" Ethan said with a smile. "You crazy . . . lucky . . . bastard."

"All guts and all glory," Ken said. "I was there, man. You know Cap. And watch your mouth, there's a lady in the room."

"Cortland?" Ryan rasped.

"He has a broken pelvis from the fall but he's recovering nicely," Mia said, stroking Ryan's hair.

"He and I wouldn't be here if you hadn't come for us."

"The lady's right, Cap," Ethan said, smoothing a palm over his five o'clock shadow. "Maaan . . . it was sick. Heard the team that got to Abdulla's sister's store startled him while he was in the back listening to XM radio. He rabbited, was out like a shot, and our team in the alley was in hot pursuit when he reached inside his jacket. Our guys thought he was pulling a weapon, and it wasn't until he was dead on the ground that they saw the cell phone. Everybody immediately knew the deal and started yelling to get word to call you and Ken back . . . but they said before they could dial, they heard the blast from where they were. It shattered windows for blocks." Ethan stopped and swallowed hard. "Your rusty ass is a sight for sore eyes, Captain, is all I'ma say—pardon the language, ma'am . . . but . . ."

"No apologies," Mia murmured. "I salute that sentiment, too."

"You're not the only one," Ken said, shaking his head. "The moment we opened the trunk to get Cortland out of the vehicle, we saw the squares of dynamite in duct tape, and we knew we were cooked. All we could do was pray we could outrun it. Ryan grabbed the old man by one side; I had him by the other, trying to get behind something. Until the world stopped shaking, neither one of us knew we were alive, much less hurt."

"How long?" Ryan looked up at Mia, who seemed to know how to read his mind.

"Three days, baby. Three of the longest days in my life." She kissed his head again. "Your mother only left to go to the cafeteria with my mom a little while ago because we promised to stay here with you every second until she and your cousin came back. Camille had to work extra hard with my mom to even get her to take a sip of coffee. You were in surgery for nine hours."

"You'll be outta here in no time, bro." Ethan gave him a big smile. "They just had to take out like a foot of intestines, but all your vitals are good. What's a little steel to the gizzard for a man of Delta Force, Hoo-ah!"

"Hoo-ah!" Ken said, laughing.

Ethan bumped chests with Ken and then turned to Mia and gave her a wink. "Don't let him use that Purple Heart injury as a reason to wiggle out of the nuptials."

Mia laughed. "I not letting his asset of value get away, believe that, gentlemen."

"Don't worry, Lieutenant, I'm not going AWOL on this one," Ryan said, his voice still gravelly as he gazed up at Mia with a smile. "But I do need one of you guys to bust me out of here soon so I can go get a ring."

EPILOGUE

*Five months later,
U.S. Military Academy at West Point . . .*

Ryan stood at attention at the front of Holy Trinity
Church in his dress uniform, eyes straight ahead,
chin lifted, waiting. He hadn't been back to West
Point since he'd graduated and taken a solemn oath.
Now he was back and would be taking another
deeply personal oath. Again, this one for life.

But this time around, ten years made all the difference in the world as he looked out at his nieces
and nephews and all his boys. However, some
things hadn't changed. His mother was crying, just
like before. He'd thought he was going to have to
give her smelling salts when Mia had asked if it
would be all right to get married here. He loved his
bride all the more because of it. And just like before, he hated the wait to see Mia again, the jitters

in his stomach as time stretched out and yawned, in no hurry at all.

And this time of year the campus truly strutted her stuff in breathtaking gold, red, and fire orange hues. It was as though the academy had put on its formal dress uniform just to make Mia smile. Up until now the cherry blossoms of spring always made him wax nostalgic. But today he'd go to his grave swearing that late September was his preferred season. Mia changed everything and always made him deeply philosophical, always had even when she didn't know it.

But there was absolutely no way to remain philosophical when the music began. Didn't matter that he'd been in mortal combat or hellhole dogfights. This feeling was new, turned him inside out. He was glad that his boys Ken and Ethan had his back, along with Mia's brother, because how did a man prepare himself to see his woman turn into an angel right before his eyes?

Each of her two bridesmaids came down the aisle first, making the wait a little longer, obstructing his view in their deep fall red and burnt orange hues. Her sister seemed to understand. Elyse smiled at him and gave him a quick nod. Her cousin almost giggled. Then he had to wait for her girl, Camille, to make the solo maid-of-honor stroll wearing dark gold. Then her little cousin, who was only about three years old, had to be coaxed to walk out in front of everyone, which broke the tension and made everybody laugh.

That was a dangerous thing in the long run, because it left him slightly off guard and completely vulnerable when Mia finally appeared under the arch next to Dr. Cortland. The old man lifted his chin with tears in his eyes and took his sweet time, managing careful steps forward on a cane. They shared a look, a thanks that never had to be said. And then old man Cortland brought him his bride.

She floated toward him on a mirage of ivory chiffon. A simple scoop neck framed her bosom, and a wide sash that tied under her breasts in a bow of dark gold satin flowed as she took each step. The bottom her dress fanned out all around her and hid her feet. Pearls were in her upswept hair and teardrops of pearls hung from her delicate earlobes. Her mouth was that same color peach that had blown him away the first time, and everything about her face was exquisite serenity.

He swallowed hard as he saw her bouquet quiver. He wanted to go to her so badly, to hold her and tell her everything was going to be fine. She was perfect, so the day was perfect as far as he was concerned. As long as she became his wife right now, today, none of the pomp and circumstance mattered.

But he knew he was a man of no frills and used to stripped-down combat conditions. He would have married her on a street corner in Brazil—he didn't care. Could've gone to the justice of the peace, since she was definitely concerned about time. But she wanted a church wedding, and he respected that. The fact that it mattered to her so deeply made it vitally important to him.

She'd been so stressed about the time, about her growing baby bump, which to his way of looking at it was the most beautiful thing on her. Time had moved her to tears, and he'd moved heaven and earth to get a date that she could live with . . . all because it mattered to her. But what she didn't understand was that he was so proud of that bump. He remembered every detail of how his son got put there, right before a mission that could have taken Mia's life.

He also remembered how time was merciful and had allowed a homeless man to give him the rest of a good life. He owed time a lot; owed the good Lord even more. He'd be making regular visits to help LeRoy and people like him who'd lost their way. Had to make time for people trapped outside normal time. That was also the one thing he never wanted to happen to him again—to miss out on all the wonderful things time offered.

Watching Mia come down the aisle he wondered about pieces of his life that he'd never thought about before, like whether or not he could be gone when this new life came . . . whether he could stand missing the chance to throw out a baseball or teach his boy to dribble. Wondered if he could take as many risks now, knowing what it would do to those he'd leave behind. Yes, he still wanted to make the world safer, but maybe Ian Cortland and his mother's sage words were right: There was a time for every season. Maybe he'd been wrong and it was true that Mia made him even more philosophical now than she did a long time ago.

Mia came to his arm as his best man helped Dr. Cortland to his seat. Ken looked so serious when he came back to his position beside him. Their eyes met. Maybe his best buddy could tell that something profound had just shifted in time. Both mothers were twisting tissues, and everyone in the church seemed to be miles away. And Mia was so beautiful that he almost forgot the order of the service and lifted her veil to kiss her.

But the priest cleared his throat. That drew laughs from the pews and made Mia laugh behind her hand.

"We're not at that part yet, son."

"Sorry, sir," Ryan said quietly. But his gaze never left Mia's face.

He'd been time confused, wasted time, but in the final hours he knew just how precious time was. As he stood there and the priest read words he was barely listening to, he was working on a way to say thank you to God and to share his time with the world in a slightly different way.

His yet-to-be-born son, just like all the kids in the audience, needed a chance to be his best. That took time. His own father had never put in the time; he'd always vowed that he would when it was his turn. The job that Ian Cortland was willing to create at the Smithsonian to help minority kids get interested in science was looking better by the second. His cover story could be made into a reality.

When Ryan briefly scanned the audience, Colonel Mitchell gave him a nod from the pews and released what seemed to be a solemn sigh. Maybe that old war dog also knew it was time. It was amazing how time changed perspectives and opened new doors while old ones closed.

This time when the minister cleared his throat, Ryan simply looked up at the man. He hadn't a clue as to where they were in the ceremony. Ken wasn't handing him the ring—so where were they?

"Do you, or don't you, take this woman to be your lawfully wedded wife?"

"Affirmative," Ryan said, much louder than he'd intended.

The priest laughed with the audience. "Good, because the pause had us worried, son."

"No worries, sir," his best man said, landing a supportive hand on Ryan's shoulder. "After what this man went through to get her, trust me, he's locked and loaded and fully committed. Hoo-ah!"

The wedding devolved from that point. Mia threw back her veil and kissed him hard, laughing. Loud cheers and the military *Hoo-ah* rang through the chapel—and nobody cared how long a time it took to bring enough order to finish the rest of the ceremony.

Miami, Florida . . . Present Day

Sage stood under the intense, multi-head shower spray, scrubbing her body with expensive shower gel until her skin felt raw. She'd definitely crossed the line. Other DEA Special Agents had warned her that it always came down to this when working on a long, involved undercover investigation. They'd told her to "get her head right" and to be ready, because there'd always be a point of no return when one had to decide how much of oneself you were willing to give for your country, willing to do to fit into the dark and decadent underbelly of illegal drugs.

The men who had preceded her on the case had gone in as deal makers, distributors, security forces, all in an attempt to trick Roberto Salazar into giving them access to his inner workings. But Salazar was no fool and each attempt by agents before her had gotten them close, but never close enough . . . until she'd entered the scene.

Before this assignment, she'd thought she could handle it. She didn't think she had a line. Her field division supervisor had kept asking her if she was prepared, and she'd repeatedly told him yes without blinking or stuttering. She'd wanted this. She'd hounded Hank Wilson until he'd given her the plum assignment. Drug kingpins from the infamous Salazar Brothers Alliance had created the chain of events that had left her mother and younger brother, along with her baby sister, dead—mowed down by ricocheted bullets in a territorial dispute. She had more at stake in this than anyone in the department. That was her trump card that finally got Hank to relent.

Innocents had bled to death in front of a corner grocery store. The Salazars' careless bullets had left her grandmother wailing in a hospital, on her knees in prayer, begging doctors to revive DOA incoming. These same ruthless killers had left her grandmother stranded by grief in church, screaming over caskets . . . and had left her traumatized and mute when authorities collected her from North Miami High School to tell that, save her Nana, everyone in her immediate family was dead.

Yeah, she'd lobbied for the assignment.

With her eyes closed, Sage turned off the water with an unsteady grip, wondering how her life had become so completely screwed up by thirty years old.

None of this was in her personal plan. She reached for a thick, Turkish bath sheet and pressed her face into the fragrant knap of the towel, remembering how she'd thought she could change things the second she'd graduated from Miami U with a B.S. in Criminal Justice, determined to be a part of the war on drugs. That seemed so far away now.

Sage let out a sad sigh and began drying off her body. Back then, women new to law enforcement held up Michele Leonhart as the consummate role model. Even to this day she still was that, and oddly had just been appointed to the DEA's Senior Executive Service to spearhead special agent recruitment efforts at DEA Headquarters the same year Sage's family had been killed, 1996. Leonhart had broken through the glass ceiling and was a glass ceiling breaker, she was a woman who had it all . . . two kids, a husband, and was a sterling example of law enforcement. Her idol was a woman who'd worked her way up in the agency from a beat cop in Minnesota to finally be unanimously confirmed as the deputy administrator of the DEA by the U.S. Senate. Leonhart was everything that she had once wanted to be, while also seeming to have the American dream to go along with it.

But Sage was now pretty sure that her idol didn't own the dark need for vengeance that she did, and probably hadn't gone fully undercover to this degree. Although she didn't know for sure, she was fairly certain that Leonhart had stayed on the cleaner side of investigations.

Not looking in the foggy wall-to-ceiling mirrors, Sage walked over to the large, white marble sink and pumped body lotion into her hand. Nana had warned that unless she released her hatred of those who had killed her momma and siblings, one day it would destroy her soul. She used to scoff at that warning, unable to explain to her grandmother that more than revenge fueled her ambition. Fear ruled it.

It was impossible to just sit idly by and watch what happened to her happen to other families. Her worst nightmares had come true as she witnessed the rising statistics of drug-related violence. Men like Roberto Salazar were getting stronger, not weaker. More families were grieving over innocent blood spilled than ever before. Being paralyzed by the threat of retaliation was more than her soul could bear . . . it was an ongoing violation of her spirit until the day she decided that, if she wasn't a part of the solution, she was part of the problem. Someone had to address the tide of destruction that had become a national tsunami. Given that she had nothing left to lose other than her life, who better to get involved but her?

When her Nana would try to quote scripture to dissuade her, Sage would remind her that somewhere it had said an eye for an eye and a tooth for a tooth. Nana never understood the full extent of her rage. It started off as very focused on her own personal pain and then, as time went on and story after sad story in her community happened, the rage blossomed. Sage sighed and applied more lotion.

Anger had been productive. Sage applied mineral-based anti-aging cream to her cheeks in gentle strokes. The powerful emotion had fueled her through college to graduate at the top of her class, and had rocketed her through the grueling requirements of the police academy. Rage and determination got her through the insanely competitive process of becoming a special agent . . . got her through sixteen intense weeks of training at Quantico. But maybe her Nana had been right, God rest her soul.

Sage stared in the mirror for a moment, glad that it was still opaque, and then twisted her long mass of freshly shampooed hair up into a mound on her head and clipped it in place.

Every one of her colleagues drew the line at killing an innocent human being to prove one's allegiance to the criminal they were trailing . . . but sleeping with the enemy or getting high with a target was par for the course. Blending in was paramount for survival. Her fellow veteran agents had said it wasn't until she'd been initiated, truly experienced the gut-wrenching decision of total immersion into that world, that she'd really gone undercover.

She'd definitely been initiated these last few

months. Right now she was way undercover, bordering on being in too deep. Never had she imagined that she'd have to go this far to exact the kind of justice her soul demanded. But there was no use in dwelling on it. Maybe she didn't have a soul anymore. She wasn't sure if it had fled her the day they'd told her that her family had been slain.

The one thing she was certain of, however, was that Roberto Salazar was about to do a mega deal with Anwar Assad. The Miami drug alliance was about to bring in major weight from Afghanistan. A link with al-Qaeda was firmly established due to her expertly placed bugs; getting close to Salazar gave her free access to the ten-thousand-square-foot mansion, Salazar's marina, as well as the seventy-seven thousand square feet of opulently manicured, waterfront grounds that surrounded his Miami compound.

Now her field division knew for sure that drugs flowing through Miami via a newly expected shipment were going to fund a large arms buy—weapons from a Canadian source to be used against U.S. troops. The DEA's foreign-deployed advisory and support teams had echoed that intel. Her objective now that she'd gotten in close with Salazar was to find where the drop would take place, where the money was going to be wired, and who the Canadian arms contact was so they could hot the bastards.

Sage stared in the mirror full on now, watching the steam slowly dissipate. Hell, yeah, putting her body on the line was worth it. Others had taken shrapnel or a bullet or a roadside bomb. She looked at her blurry image without blinking. Yes, she could continue this mission through to the bitter end, no matter what it took . . . not only for her family and for all those grieving families who had been caught in the crosshairs of drug violence, but for every person—military or civilian—who had been slain by terrorism.

"Small price to pay," she murmured and then turned away from the mirror to gather her sunscreen. Everything about her life now was a lie and the lines between who she'd been and who she was were as blurry as the bathroom mirror.

So what that in order to get in, she'd had to play the role of Salazar's lover? It didn't matter that the moment when she'd been accepted into her target's inner circle and into his heart, she'd been forced to mentally separate from herself. If she was to be Salazar's woman, then she had to sleep with him. Period. But it wasn't her; the new identity took over. It was the only way she could do what she'd had to do. Special Agent Sage Wagner was now completely Camille Rodriguez, a biracial Latina . . . part African American and Latino, lover and numero-uno girlfriend of Roberto Salazar. Whatever it took, she'd use to get in close to complete her mission.

She looked up calmly as the bathroom door opened, tucking away her innermost thoughts. A cool shaft of air rushed in with Roberto, sunlight framing his six-foot-two, athletic build. He had on a classic business suit: navy-blue pin-striped, single-breasted Armani with a French blue, white-collared shirt, paisley silk tie, and seeming quite the dignified business man. He was on his way to Miami International Airport to meet with Assad . . . but where were they headed after that?

"I thought you were going to wash yourself down the drain." Roberto beamed at her and openly appraised her towel-clad form.

She tilted her head and offered him a pout. "No, just getting ready to go shopping . . . Are you still going to your meeting alone or can you take me this time? I can read a magazine or amuse myself in the cafes or shops wherever you're going for a couple of hours until you're finished. Come on, Roberto. I'm bored. After you're done, we could do something fun."

"It has been a while since we've done something fun," he murmured, his eyes stripping away the towel. "I admit that I've been preoccupied with business lately . . . but it won't always be this way."

"After your meeting, we could go out . . . or . . . not."

She offered him a sexy half-smile and waited. When he hesitated and didn't immediately respond, she moved toward him slowly, studying his handsome smile and intense dark eyes, allowing his freshly barbered hair to thread through her fingers once she'd reached him. It had been several weeks since he'd touched her; the negotiations were obviously taking a toll on his libido—which was a good thing and a bad thing. Much could be extricated from him if he was still interested in her, a lot could be learned in pillow talk or while he spoke to his colleagues on the phone while in the bedroom. But lately he'd been aloof, and that wasn't good.

She then leaned up and into him to brush his mouth with a kiss. "You took too long to answer me, so I already know the answer."

He circled her waist with his hands, caressing it through the damp towel. "I took too long to answer you because I was deciding, *corazon*. You make it hard for a man to think about business." He kissed her deeply and then drew away. "But to keep you in fashion and in this mansion, there are certain things I cannot neglect . . . *sì?*"

Hating that he'd tied her to his illicit deals, even if it was through the temporarily lavish lifestyle he shared with her or whatever other fantasy he'd concocted in his mind, she nodded and released a long, faux-submissive sigh. "*Sì.*"

Fort Bragg, North Carolina . . .

Captain Anthony Davis sat transfixed as his battalion commander gave his unit the briefing. The next generation of Salazar drug traffickers was expanding well beyond their Miami operations, making alliances with Afghan and Pakistan nationals that had known ties to both the Taliban and al-Qaeda. Satellite photos of the Salazar compound flashed across the briefing room screen.

"We've got seventy-seven thousand square feet exposed with a hundred and eighty-degree view of the water. This place was arrogantly built for luxury, not built to withstand a fast, pre-emptive strike," Colonel Mitchell said, looking around the small Delta Force unit. "Cabanas, pool, tennis courts, marina . . . all make good access points and hiding places, but don't get sloppy. Make no mistake, this compound is heavily armed, even though it seems fairly spread out and easy to wire. If the targets fall back to this position—which hopefully they will with all of Assad's people—I'd rather you go in and take them down the old-fashioned way, rather than leave a smoking black hole in this otherwise upscale, residential neighborhood. The main house is a ten-thousand-square-foot, seven-bedroom, seven-bathroom monstrosity that will leave quite an eyesore if you have to blow it."

"No trouble with the Posse Commitatus Act, Colonel?" Captain Davis asked carefully, and then glanced at Lieutenants Butcher and Hayes.

"No," Colonel Mitchell said in a flat tone. "We are in hot pursuit from our units in Afghanistan. That voids our concern about getting caught in a jurisdictional battle with the Drug Enforcement Administration or any other stateside law enforcement organization. We have word from the DEA through our International Joint Task Force on Homeland Security that the same target we have, Anwar Assad, is doing a deal in DEA's Miami jurisdiction. We are getting more intel as we speak from their field division special agents, and we're eventually going to need to establish a liaison relationship between us and the DEA. But right now, we're burning daylight. You better than anyone know that we cannot waste time with bureaucratic bull. We have to strike while the iron is hot. So, although our roles somewhat overlap on this one, our mission is clear."

The colonel began slowly pacing at the front of the briefing room, ticking off the points on his thick fingers as he enumerated them for his men. "One—confiscate the shipment to keep that insane amount of narcotics off our American streets; two—via Central Intelligence, our forces are to track all funds transfers so we can cast a wider net to catch even bigger fish, and so we can interrupt the cash flow of this operation to cripple it; and three—capture the bastards for future intel if we can, or exterminate them on site if we can't. Allowing any of them to disappear back into the shadows or to hide behind the facade of being legitimate businessmen isn't an option. They're attempting to bring the party to our house, so, gentlemen, let's show 'em a real good time."

"Roger that," Captain Davis replied, staring at

the beautiful woman who had briefly graced the screen. "How much civilian collateral damage is at risk within the compound, sir?"

"We're not sure at this time, because the household population changes daily based on who-ever is visiting. That's why it's an option of last re-sort, but one that may be ultimately necessary—so rig it." Colonel Mitchell clasped his hands behind his back and lifted his chin, but his eyes were troubled. "There may be a few girlfriends and non-security civilian staff inside the compound when the time comes . . . which is regrettable and also why I'm giving you orders to rig it for detonation as a last resort, but to preferably go in as a small, swift-moving assassin squad. It's always unfortu-nate to have civilian losses, but sometimes it's un-avoidable."

"Understood, sir," Captain Davis said, glancing at his lieutenants, who nodded, and then returned his attention to the colonel.

Although he outwardly seemed engaged in the colonel's words, in truth he was momentarily un-able to get the image of the shapely, bikini-clad, cocoa-skinned woman with a million-dollar smile out of his head. He oddly found himself wondering what her eyes looked like behind the huge, black designer sunglasses she wore, and wanted to know how a woman who appeared so classy could wind up sleeping with a drug kingpin.

But just as immediately as the thought flitted

through his mind, he banished it. Women like that did anything for money, and that same beauty would be the first one to put a bullet in his skull if she thought he was going to try to capture or kill her lover.

A long deployment in Afghanistan without regular female companionship was probably what was wearing on him, if he'd gotten temporarily distracted from a mere photo. Would have been nice to get one more quick trip in to Amsterdam for some paid brothel talent before he'd had to track Assad, but that was the last thing he needed to be thinking about at the moment.

Anthony immediately admonished himself. He was stateside now, just had to complete this mission, then he'd be able to have a life for a couple of weeks.